2

A Walk on the Dead Side

Cover by Lewellen Designs
Editing by Angie Ramey

A WALK ON
THE DEAD SIDE

Secret Seal Isle

Book 3

LUCY QUINN

1.

———————————————

"COOKIE!" RAIN CALLED as she ran from the kitchen, her bright red hair sticking out at all angles.

"What the heck happened to you?" Cookie James asked, pausing in front of the front door of the inn she owned. She took a good long look at her mother, noting the smudged eye makeup and mud-stained, silver-sequined dress. It was quite the sight for any woman, much less one in her late sixties.

"Not what happened, dear. It's who." Her mother pumped her eyebrows suggestively. "You remember that silver fox who checked in over the weekend?"

"Mother." Cookie took a deep breath, trying to keep her irritation in check. "You didn't."

"Oh, I did. Over and over and over again. He did this thing with his—"

"Stop!" Cookie covered her ears with her hands. "Please keep the details of your bedroom gymnastics to yourself. No daughter wants to hear her mother talk about… well you know, this stuff."

"Oh, we weren't in the bedroom," Rain said with a sly smile.

"Gah!" Cookie pulled the door open and stepped out on the wrap-around porch, nearly running straight into the wide chest of Dylan Creed, the man who was there to pick her up for their raincheck date.

"Well, good morning," he said, steadying her with his large hands.

Her breath caught as she looked up into his handsome face. Dark eyes smiled down on her. "Um, morning."

"Oh, don't you look handsome today," Rain gushed, pushing Cookie aside.

"Rain," he said with a polite nod. "You look… ah, like you had a good time last night."

Rain giggled, a slight blush staining her cheeks. "Last night *and* this morning. I needed to give our guest a warm send off."

Dylan choked out a laugh. "Is that what you're calling it these days?"

"Oh, hell," Cookie muttered. "Dylan, we better get going otherwise we'll end up with an x-rated play-by-play." She grabbed his hand and started tugging him down the porch stairs.

"Wait!" Rain called running after them. "You're going to need these."

Cookie stopped and turned back just in time to see Rain pulled a couple of square, foil-wrapped condom packages out of her cleavage. Horror filled her as she prayed the earth would open up and swallow her whole. Maybe if Cookie ignored her, Dylan wouldn't notice. "We're good. Thanks anyway, mother." Cookie tightened her grip on Dylan's hand, moving toward his truck. They had a picnic to get to.

"Safety first!" Rain said, rushing to Cookie's side. She pressed the packages into Cookie's hand. "No sense getting caught out in the rain without a *rain*coat. Get it?" She cackled at her joke.

With her face burning, Cookie quickly shoved the protection into her shorts pocket and glared at her mother.

But Rain glanced down at the ground. "Oops. You dropped one."

Cookie cut her gaze to the blue wrapper, swore under her breath, then glanced at Dylan.

He was grinning like a loon, but to his credit, he didn't say anything. He just reached down, picked up the condom, and nodded to her mother. "Thanks, Rain. You're right. One never can be too prepared."

"Someone kill me now," Cookie muttered.

"Na." Dylan held the condom up and winked at her. "We wouldn't want these to go to waste would we?"

"That's the spirit, dear," Rain said, patting his arm. "Now you two kids go have some fun. Cookie could use a good—"

"Mother!" Cookie admonished.

Rain held up her hands. "I'm just saying."

Dylan laughed, put the condom in his back pocket, then guided Cookie to his truck. "Come on. Lunch is waiting."

❧

COOKIE, UNABLE TO get the condom incident out of her mind, was mostly silent as Dylan navigated his boat out of Secret Seal harbor. She knew he wasn't expecting anything from her. They barely had a relationship. But still... knowing there was a condom burning a hole in both of their pockets had sent her imagination into a tailspin. She cleared her throat, ready to tackle to incident head-on, but then he spoke, ignoring the subject entirely.

"So you were a spy."

Cookie sighed, both wary and relieved at the out-of-the-blue question. She sat up a little, shading her eyes with one hand so she could study her accuser. The sun was warm on her face as her heart started to jackhammer with pleasure. Dylan was grinning at her, dimples on full attack, steel-blue eyes crinkling at the corners and glinting with mischief.

"Sure," she replied after a second, feeling her own lips tug upward in a smirk. "That was me, a regular Jane Bond."

That drew a laugh out of him, a deep, rich, rolling sound that brought a wide smile to her face. "No, but seriously," he said, keeping a steady hand on the controls of the outboard motor as they tooled around the small islands off the coast of Maine. "You've never said what you did before you moved out here. I'm guessing you weren't in the hospitality business."

"No. Running an inn is a new venture for us." Cookie's mind wandered to the Secret Seal Inn and her mother Rain, who no doubt was getting into some kind of trouble. There was no telling what Cookie would walk in on when she got home later. Hopefully it didn't involve anymore naked guests or special brownies. You'd think a hot, smart, charming, capable guy like Dylan would have every bit of Cookie's focus. But when her mind wandered to Rain, all bets were off.

"Judging by the way you handled the scene on Dickie's boat," Dylan continued, referencing the dead man they'd found with his junk tied up in a big red bow, "and the fact that Hayley said you were some kind of badass taking down those guys singlehandedly. . ." he shook his head. "It's obvious you've got some serious training going on there."

Cookie wanted to deny it, to make something up, but knew there was no point. She couldn't explain away her role in saving Hayley from would-be kidnappers. He had her dead to rights. Besides, she liked Dylan. Maybe even *really* liked him, though it was a little early to tell. But she definitely liked him enough that she didn't want to have to lie to him. So instead, as much as it went against both her instincts and her training, she told him the truth.

"I did train," she admitted, straightening up so she

could shift on the boat's bench seat and face him fully. "At Quantico." She offered him her hand. "Former FBI Special Agent Cookie James, pleased to meet you."

Dylan's smile said he wasn't quite sure if she was joking with the handshake, but he accepted it anyway. "FBI, huh?" he replied, his strong, slender fingers wrapping around her own hand firmly but still gently enough to send a shiver straight through her. A good shiver that had nothing to do with the cool ocean breeze blowing through her hair. "But former?" he let her go and leaned back on his own seat a little. "What happened?"

She shrugged, looking away and trying to convince someone, either him or herself, that it wasn't a big deal. "I pissed off the wrong people," she answered slowly. "It wasn't safe for me to stay, and it wasn't the kind of thing I couldn't fight, so I got the hell out."

When she looked up again, she saw he was frowning, and his eyes had darkened slightly, shading from blue toward gray. *Uh oh.* She'd already known him long enough to realize that meant he was either irritated or angry.

"Pissed off how?" he asked quietly. "When you say the wrong people, do you mean perps or peers?"

A wave of warmth rushed through her as she processed his questions. It hadn't dawned on her he'd be upset on her behalf. He thought she'd been wronged at the Bureau, and that's why she'd left. "It wasn't anyone at work, nothing like that," she hurried to assure him. "I took somebody down, but the organization is still out there, and that makes me a target. If I'd been the only one on their radar, that would've been fine, I'd have handled it. But I couldn't risk them going after anyone else to get to me."

"Your mother, Rain?" he asked.

Cookie nodded.

"Yeah, I get that," he assured her, and she thought he probably did. Which reminded her that he had a few secrets of his own.

"What about you?" She leaned forward, not missing the way his eyes flicked to the opening of her loose shirt and the bikini top that peeked through. "You told me once that you left for a few years, for school and other stuff, before coming back, but I get the feeling there's more to it than that. You've got some skills you didn't pick up on a college campus." She remembered the way he'd taken Hunter down when her former partner had tried getting in his face. Not a lot of guys could do that. And Dylan had made it look easy, almost instinctual, like he'd been thoroughly trained and on autopilot.

He held up his free hand, chuckling. "Oh, no," he told her, "we're still talking about you, Miss Federal Agent. We'll get to me some other time."

You bet I will, Cookie thought to herself, but didn't argue. Despite it being a little one-sided, she was enjoying the conversation. And the view. But not just Dylan. The sky was a pristine blue, while the glinting sun made the water appear to be a sheet of silvered glass.

Even the hum of the engine was soothing, and she found herself sighing contentedly.

Dylan flashed his easy smile. "What?"

"Nothing." She shook her head, worried that she'd sound stupid, but then blurted it out anyway. "It's just— it's nice here. Quiet. Peaceful. Beautiful." She glanced his way, peering at him through her lashes in case he was going to mock her. "I like it."

"I'm glad," he said, and sounded completely serious. "Hopefully that means you'll stick around for a while." There were those dimples again. They were so dangerous, they probably should've been registered as lethal weapons, Cookie thought, trying not to let on just how much they affected her. But then he turned serious and the dimples vanished as he asked, "You are planning to stick around, right?"

"Absolutely," she answered. "Why wouldn't I?" She made a point of glancing around and then eyed him hungrily. "What else could a girl possibly need?"

She was pleased to see that she'd gotten him to blush, at least. But that wasn't enough to distract him from the topic. "You're not planning to go back to the FBI once things are settled at home?"

Cookie frowned. She wanted to just tell him no, of course not. But he appeared serious about the question, and it deserved a proper, honest answer. "I'm not saying there aren't things I miss about Philly," she admitted.

He nodded. "Sure. That's understandable. Moving to a new place is hard."

"Right. So, yeah, there are things I miss there. People, too. But I don't know that I can go back. Things have changed. I've changed." She thought about her old life and her old self. About how driven she'd been, and how she'd been determined to show everyone a woman could do the job just as well as a man. She'd succeeded, but she'd sacrificed every other area of her life getting there. Cookie hadn't minded at the time. She'd loved her job. But now... she wasn't so sure it was worth it.

She shook her head, sending a lock of her thick auburn waves across her cheek and into her eyes. Pushing it back, she once again met his contemplative gaze. "This place has a way of getting its hooks into a person, you know? I never thought I'd say this, but I kind of love it here. The simplicity, the beauty, and despite all her crazy antics, I *might* even be enjoying spending more time with Rain."

"You've only been here, what, a month?" Dylan asked, still frowning slightly. "A little more?" After she nodded, he continued. "And already you've gotten caught up in *two* murder investigations."

"Neither of which turned out to be murders, exactly," Cookie pointed out. The first one had proven to be an accidental death, and the second had been a natural death, just unexpected and linked to a blackmail plot.

"Sure, but the point is, you always seem to be where the action is," Dylan said. "I just don't know if you're as ready for the quiet life as you claim, that's all."

"Well, you'd better keep me entertained then, hadn't you?" she shot back, batting her eyelashes at him, feeling slightly foolish. She wasn't normally this...*bold*.

That got him to laugh again. "Sure, you say that, but it took me a week to get you out here," he reminded her.

"Hey, that isn't all on me," she shot back. "I seem to recall somebody else begging off a few times, too."

"Guilty as charged," Dylan agreed, still smiling. "What was I to do? Mrs. Ledger's basement was flooded, and it couldn't wait." As the town's one and only handyman, Dylan got called for all kinds of odd jobs and repairs. But Cookie could tell he loved it. Still, between his work and her dealing with the inn and her mom, it had taken until today before they'd both had any free time.

"We're here now," she said, leaning against the side of the boat again. She tilted her head back a little and closed her eyes as a spray of cool water splashed on her face. "I figure it was worth the wait."

"Oh, no argument there," she heard Dylan murmur, and smiled. Even with her eyes shut, Cookie could guess from his tone that he was studying her body in her cut-off shorts and white cross-tied shirt, and that he liked what he saw.

Yes, there were definitely some things on Secret Seal Isle worth sticking around for.

2.

―――――――――――――――――――――

"WHAT DO YOU think?" Dylan asked as he drew the boat up alongside a piling and expertly looped the anchor rope around it. "Better by day?" He shut off the boat's motor and gathered the picnic basket from the bench beside him.

Cookie laughed. "Much." The last time she'd been out here to Lookout Point it had been night time, and she and Hunter had been racing to save Hayley Holloway from a blackmail scheme and potential kidnapping situation. She hadn't exactly had the time to look around and appreciate her surroundings. The threat of being shot had been a much higher priority.

Now, however, there was nobody here but them. It was broad daylight, and she could admire the island to her heart's content. It really was a nice little place. She'd noticed on her previous visit that it was mostly circular, with a ring of rocks around the edge and a gentle, grassy mound at the center. The island was small enough that as they clambered over the outer ring, she could see clear across to the other side. Add a few tables and benches and maybe a grill, and you'd have the perfect spot for a private picnic gathering.

"So, what's for lunch?" Cookie asked as she followed him toward the top of the mound.

"Lobster rolls and coleslaw from the Salty Dog. And if that isn't enough, I might have a container of berries and homemade whipped cream. Not to mention the wine. Sound good?" he asked, glancing back over his shoulder.

"It's perfect," she said, quickening her pace to catch up with him. But as she took another glance at the rocky shores, she stopped abruptly, focusing on a glint at the water's edge. That familiar sense of unease, the one that silently warned her something wasn't quite right, blossomed in her gut.

"What's that?" she asked, straightening and craning her neck for a better look. "There's something over there."

"Where?" Dylan paused and shifted to look in the direction she indicated, but then frowned. "I don't see anything."

"On the water, or near it. Looks like a piece of metal," Cookie said, not looking away as she began to move slowly toward whatever it was. "Must not be too big, because you've got to be at just the right angle to see it."

She could hear the scrape of Dylan's feet scrambling over the rocks to follow her. "I see it," he replied quietly.

Then he cursed under his breath. "Nope, lost it. It's probably just something that washed up here. It happens. The tide grabs all kinds of things."

Keeping her gaze locked on the glinting metal, Cookie rushed down to the water's edge, slipping twice on the loose stone, only to be caught both times by Dylan's strong arms. It wasn't exactly a hardship. She'd thanked him both times, but didn't let her hormones deter her.

Finally, she stood on a broad, flat rock that jutted out over the water. Seagulls called out as they flew overhead, and at her feet she spotted the object of her journey. It was metal, all right. A large metal cage, to be precise, with a hinged door along one side and a latched top. The whole thing was made of thick, sturdy mesh, most of it covered in a protective coating of some sort. What she'd seen had been spots where that coating had recently rubbed or scraped off, leaving shiny metal beneath.

She knew what it was, of course. You didn't live on an island that still counted lobstering as its major industry without having seen plenty of these. It was a lobster trap, only it didn't have any lobsters in it.

But it was far from empty.

Instead, the cage was stuffed full of flat, rectangular packages about the size and shape of a bag of flour. Each one had been shrink-wrapped to keep it watertight, and Cookie had a pretty good idea what they contained. She'd been on enough drug busts that all it took was one look through the mesh trap to recognize the contents.

"Okay," she said, turning toward Dylan as he stopped beside her and stared down at their find. "So why would somebody fill their lobster trap with drugs? And how did the trap wind up all the way over here?" Most lobstermen weighted their traps with bricks to make sure they sank well beneath the surface where the lobsters were more likely to find them, and to keep the traps from getting tossed about by the current. It didn't look like this one had any bricks in it, though. At least, not of the building variety.

Dylan shook his head. "There have always been stories of drug running in the area." Squatting down, he studied the trap and its contents. "I guess a lobster trap would be a good way to stash the drugs somewhere, maybe for somebody else to come along and retrieve them. I don't know anybody who does that, though. The only dealer I ever knew of was Stone, and he was strictly small-time. Plus he's out of the business now…"

Stone Harris had been lucky. He'd been involved in the cover-up of a man's death, but it had been an accident. Lucky for him, he'd gotten only a fine and some community service. But it meant the local sheriff was keeping a close eye on him, and although Stone wasn't the brightest fellow, even he knew better than to try dealing while under that sort of scrutiny. "As far as how it got here…" Dylan studied the trap, then pointed to the top of the cage where an empty metal ring stood up from the surface. "No rope. Either it snapped, or it wasn't tied right, or somebody didn't even bother to lash it down. I'd guess the current got it, and it got swept along until it caught up against the rocks here." He grimaced. "Just our luck."

Cookie pulled out her cell phone. She wasn't all that surprised to see she actually had service here. With Secret Seal maybe fifteen minutes in one direction and the mainland city of Hancock twenty to thirty in the other, they had plenty of overlapping signal. She started to punch in the number for the Secret Seal Isle sheriff's office but hesitated before hitting Enter.

"What's up?" Dylan asked, twisting and leaning back to study her face.

"Oh, nothing," she started. Then she shrugged. "It's just—Deputy Swan, he's not a bad guy or anything, but he just isn't…"

"Isn't exactly Super Cop," Dylan finished for her. "Yeah, I know. He hasn't really needed to be. Not a lot of crime out here most of the time." He shrugged. "Still, he is the local law. You've got to let him know."

"I know." Cookie sighed. She couldn't stop thinking about the last time she'd seen Swan—when he'd brought her and Hunter some crucial evidence in the case they'd been investigating. Evidence that the deputy had found at the crime scene days earlier, pocketed, and then completely forgotten about. How she was supposed to call that same man and tell him about what had to be tens of thousands of dollars' worth of drugs she'd just found?

"Cookie." Dylan's voice had just a hint of warning to it. "You're *ex*-FBI, remember? He's the deputy. Call him."

"Yeah, yeah, fine." She hit Enter and the phone rang in her ear as she waited for the call to connect.

"Swan," he barked over the line.

"Deputy," she said as brightly as she could manage. "This is Cookie, Cookie James. I'm out on Lookout Point with Dylan, and we just found a lobster trap filled with drugs, and—"

"Drugs? Did you say drugs?" he sputtered, then let out an oomph as if he'd just been gut punched. "Dammit. Who left that file drawer open?" he yelled into her ear.

Cookie couldn't do it. She couldn't let Swan screw this up, and she was sure he would, so she said, "Um, yeah. Drugs. Why don't I bring the trap back to the island with me and hold onto it for safekeeping until you and Sheriff Watkins can figure out how to dispose of it?" She didn't wait for his reply. "Thanks, bye." She hung up before he could make another attempt at bursting her eardrum.

Dylan was eyeing her with a look that she interpreted as half amused and half...scandalized? Appalled? Maybe just confused? "What?" she asked, tucking her phone back in her pocket. "No sense in him coming all the way out here when we've got this handled, right?"

"Right. And you holding onto the drugs for him, that's just, what, you lending a helping hand?" He closed his eyes for a second and shook his head. "The quiet, simple life, huh?"

"I didn't go looking for a crate full of drugs," she pointed out. "It came looking for me." She smiled and patted him on the shoulder. "Now, are you going to help me carry this thing back to the boat, or not?"

Dylan grumbled something under his breath. Cookie thought she heard "bossy" and "can't leave well enough alone" and "waste of a perfectly good lunch," but he grabbed the front of the trap and tried to haul it out of the water. It barely budged.

Cookie jumped into the water, icy waves lapping at her legs as she got behind it to push. Putting her weight into it, the metal bit into her palms, but it still didn't move.

"I've got a better idea," he said after their futile effort. "Wait here. I'll bring the boat around, and we'll just drag it over the side."

"Makes sense," Cookie agreed, moving back to the shore. He turned to go, and for once she didn't watch him walk way. Instead she alternated between staring down at the trap and peering out over the water, her mind awhirl. Somebody was running drugs in her backyard. And not an amateur, not with a haul this size. So who was it? How long had they been at it? And what was she going to do about it, now that it had fallen in her lap like this?

Because one thing she knew for certain—there was no way she was walking away.

3.

AFTER USING A rope and the leverage of the boat engine to tug the trap free of the rocks, Dylan helped Cookie haul the trap close to the boat.

"This thing weighs a ton," Cookie said, wiping her brow as she eyed the drug-filled trap. Glimpses of the white packages peeked through the dark water as it sloshed through the mesh. "You ready to flex some muscle?"

He gave her a cocky grin as he swept his gaze over her. "Are you?"

"Always." Cookie reached into the water, grabbing one end of the trap. The cold water numbed her fingers. "On three?"

Dylan followed her lead and nodded.

"One, two, three!" Cookie called.

They both let out groans of exertion as they hauled the trap up. But just as they were about to pull it over the side of the boat, Cookie shifted and lost her footing. With a cry, she fell backward, the wet metal slipping from her grip as the trap came crashing over the side, bringing a tidal wave of sea water with it.

Cookie let out a shocked shout as the cold water soaked her from head to toe. "Crap! That's cold."

Dylan stood over her, his button-down shirt soaked and molded to his impressive frame. "Are you okay?"

"Um…" she stared at the outline of his torso and unconsciously licked her lips.

"Cookie?"

"Yeah?" She tore her gaze away from his mouthwatering abs, and glanced up at him.

"You dropped something." He pointed to the space beside her.

She followed his gaze and spotted the blue foil-wrapped condom she'd shoved in her pocket after her mother had embarrassed the heck out of her. "Oh, hell." She reached for it, but Dylan was faster.

He grabbed it, held it up for a second, and then said, "I'll just keep this safe for now. You never know what we might need if we ever get past a first date." He let his gaze travel down her body once more before pocketing the condom and returning to the boat's controls.

Cookie glanced down at herself, noting that her white shirt was now soaked through, and said a silent thanks that she'd decided to wear a bikini and not that see-through lace bra she'd been saving for a special occasion. The first time Dylan got a glimpse of her assets, she planned to have a use for Rain's protection.

She brushed the hair out of her eyes and took a seat

across from Dylan. As he maneuvered the boat back toward Secret Seal Isle, she turned her attention to the drug-filled trap. Her brain whirled with possible drug routes and cartels and dealers. And as a result, she barely noticed when her companion stripped off his wet shirt.

Though she *had* made a note of it.

"Here." Dylan interrupted her thoughts and handed her one of the forgotten lobster rolls. "You might as well eat something, since we missed our picnic."

Cookie bit back a wince as she took the wrapped package. "Thanks. Sorry our date was ruined… again."

"Don't worry about it," he said, but she didn't miss the slight edge of disappointment in his tone.

"We'll get it right one of these days," she said, and took a bite of the lobster roll.

But he just nodded.

They rode the rest of the way back without speaking, something Cookie only realized after they'd docked. "Sorry," she told Dylan again as he pulled the boat up beside the pier at its normal slip. "Guess I'm a little distracted."

"Ya think?" he replied, but one eyebrow rose, as did the corners of his mouth. "I guess a whole crate full of drugs will do that to a girl, huh?"

"Yeah, not really my cup of tea," she retorted, "but—" She stopped mid-comeback as her mind jumped ahead a few inferences and began blaring warnings. "Oh, crap."

"What?" She must have had quite a look on her face, because Dylan went from amused to alarmed in nothing flat. "What's wrong?"

"I told Swan I'd keep these at my place." She managed not to groan too much. "At the Inn." She could tell by Dylan's expression that he wasn't getting it. "With my mom."

"Ah." That was all he said, but it was enough.

Yeah. *Ah.*

An entire crate full of drugs. Stored in the same building as her mom, Rain Forest, a woman who had once described Woodstock as "a nice quiet weekend with a few close friends." A woman who had recently started a side business making and selling hash brownies, weed lollies, and other druggie treats. A woman who had launched this new enterprise by buying the entire stock off a drug dealer who had ended up being arrested only hours later, though admittedly, not for drugs. A woman who had a very fuzzy concept of personal space, private property, and other "fiddly little legalities."

Ah was about right.

"What the hell am I going to do?" Cookie demanded, as much to herself as to Dylan. "If she catches even a hint of this stuff, it'll be as good as gone."

"Even though it's evidence?" he asked, but quickly threw up both hands in surrender. "Sorry, forget I asked."

She really worried about her facial expressions sometimes. "There's no way I can store this stuff." Cookie bit down on her bottom lip, thinking. An instant later, she turned her most winning smile on her companion.

But Dylan wasn't having any of that. "Oh, no," he said, laughing as he leaned away from her. "No way. You're the one who told Swan you'd hang onto the drugs instead of turning them over, so this is all on you. I'm out of it." He rose to his feet and they tapped lightly on the wooden planks as he hopped easily across to the dock. "I'll help you haul it back to the Inn, but that's it."

"Such a gentleman," Cookie grumbled as she got up to follow him, but deep down she knew he was right. She'd done this to herself, and it wasn't fair to expect him to bail her out of it. She'd have to do that all on her own.

Dylan had driven to the docks, so with some brute strength, they tossed the lobster trap into the back of his old pickup and then drove back up to the Inn. Pulling up before her home and business, Cookie found herself admiring the old building yet again. It really was a beautiful place, a full Victorian with its wide front porch, side turret, peaked roof, and carved posts. She'd never lived in a place as old as this, but its age lent it grandeur rather than squalor. The house had been a bit rundown when she and Rain had bought it, but even so it had carried an air of elegance that you don't find in newer homes. And of course Dylan had already helped immensely in restoring the old beauty to her former glory.

The tailgate of Dylan's truck thudded open. He groaned as we lifted the lobster trap and carried it up the steps and onto the front porch, setting the wire cage down near the Inn's front door. "You got it from here?" he asked.

"I guess I'll have to," Cookie shot back, then mentally scolded herself. It really was her own fault and her own mess. Dylan had helped a great deal by getting it back here for her. "Sorry. Yeah, I'm good. Thanks. Really."

He grinned and tossed her a half-salute as he climbed back into his truck. He'd barely pulled away before Cookie had her phone out again. This time, the number was one she knew by heart.

"Hey," she said when the recipient picked up. "It's me."

"Hey, me," he replied. "What, do you miss me already?"

"Something like that." She eyed the object near her, and its contents. "I'm currently staring at a lobster trap filled with what looks like high-grade coke. At least a dozen kilos, maybe more. Found it floating in the water by Lookout Point, hauled it back here and I'm waiting on Swan or Watkins to come check it out. Thought you should know." She waited as he laughed into the phone. It took a good twenty seconds before he regained enough control to speak.

"I'd ask if you were kidding, but there's no way you'd call just to make a joke about that," he said finally. "Right?"

"Right."

She heard him sigh. "Fine. I'm on the next plane out. Don't do anything stupid until I get there."

"Wouldn't dream of it," she promised. "I'll save all the stupid for you." Then she paused. "Thanks."

"Of course."

He hung up, and Cookie pocketed her phone. Already she felt a little better. Hunter was a damn good FBI agent. He was also her former partner, and still her friend. Though he'd made it clear he wanted to be much more, or at the very least friends with benefits. Large portions of Cookie's brain and other parts of her anatomy were still outraged that she'd thus far not agreed to the suggestion.

Now that she knew Hunter was on the way, Cookie relaxed a little. Once he got here, Hunter would be able to help her keep Rain away from the drugs. But she still had at least a day and probably more like two before he arrived.

One of the reasons she and Rain had picked Secret Seal Isle was because it was isolated. Great when you're hiding from a revenge-obsessed mobster, not so spectacular when you're desperately waiting for help to arrive. Which meant she'd have to find a way to hide the drugs from her mother. At least until Hunter got here, or until Swan or Watkins came to collect the evidence. But where was she going to hide twelve kilos of drugs in the house her mother knew at least as well as she did?

Okay, Cookie thought, studying the trap. *First things first. I can't carry all of them and the trap, there's just no way. I've got to get them out of there.* It took a little fiddling to get the trap's top undone. Rust stained her fingers before she was able to swing the top panel up and out of the way, exposing all of wrapped drug packages. *Bingo*, she thought, grinning as she pulled a kilo free.

Now what? She could get all of the drugs out of the trap, sure. But how was she going to be able to smuggle them into the house? And where would she put them? Until she could figure that out, Cookie decided to leave the drugs where they were. All except the one kilo she already had in her hand, which she kept for gauging size. Spotting an old throw draped over the back of the wicker couch, she snatched it up and shook it out. Then she turned the trap up on its side and tossed the throw over it.

Voila, instant end table! By pushing and shoving, the trap scraped across the porch as she managed to get it over and against the end of the couch where it was just another piece of furniture. That would have to do for now.

The one remaining kilo in hand, Cookie carefully opened the screen door and silently slid inside. Now, where could she hide the thing? The first place she decided to try was the office, even though she already knew that probably wouldn't work. After all, she shared the space with Rain, which meant her mother was in and out of there multiple times every day. But it was right here on the ground floor, and worth a shot.

The office wasn't heavily furnished, just a pair of

desks, a pair of desk chairs, an old wooden filing cabinet, and a big, heavy wing chair. Cookie's desk was relatively neat. She thought Hunter would have been astounded to see she'd made progress in the organization department. Rain's desk, however, was pure chaos, like a diorama of a hurricane in action.

No sense even trying Rain's desk, Cookie decided. Filing cabinet, perhaps? With three long strides, she was across the floor and tugging on the cabinet's topmost drawer, causing the moisture-swollen wood to groan as she slid it open. But the drawer proved to be far from empty.

"Swell," Cookie muttered to herself as she reached in the pile and retrieved a plastic baggie filled with three generous pinches of a dark green herb that reminded her of oregano. Only she knew it wasn't any such thing.

There was only one explanation—she'd found the rest of Rain's stash. That was the last thing she needed to deal with at the moment. Biting back a curse, she shoved the Mary Jane back in the drawer and tried to forget she ever saw it.

4.

COOKIE DID A quick mental inventory of the inn and surrounding property. The shed? No, Rain had already demonstrated that she considered that her private outdoor boudoir, which was an image Cookie had been trying not to revisit. So where?

And then it came to her.

The office door creaked as she cracked it open to check the hall. Still no physical sign of her mother, though there were noises from the kitchen that suggested Rain was busy. Good.

Moving as quietly as she could, Cookie slunk across the hall toward the stairs, but instead of heading to the second floor, she continued along the narrow hallway, stopping at a small door that led to an excellent storage space. All Cookie had been able to think when she'd first seen it was *just the right size for an underage wizard*, but she hadn't actually wound up using it, which meant it should be nice and empty. And she'd barely remembered the space was here, so hopefully Rain had forgotten about it completely.

The door didn't have a proper handle, just a small latch. Cookie pushed the little lever, hauled the door open, and froze, staring.

She blinked, unable to process what she was seeing. Had she somehow time-traveled back to the 1960s?

The little crawl space had clearly not been forgotten at all. Instead it had been fully outfitted with a thick, colorful shag carpet on the floor, a beanbag chair at either end, and a small, curving table in the middle with a lava lamp standing proudly at its center. Then when she flipped a switch, multicolored lights flickered and swirled everywhere, making her think she was on an acid trip. A bad one apparently, because it was enough to make her seasick. And the thick odor of pot permeating the tiny space certainly wasn't helping much.

Evidently Rain had claimed this little space as her private getaway.

"Never mind," Cookie muttered, stepping back and closing the small door again. She took several deep, gasping breaths of untainted air to clear both her lungs and her head. "I'll figure something else out."

She hefted the kilo she was still carrying around. With its shrink-wrapping and the white of the drug itself, it almost looked like a paper-wrapped package instead. Like a pound of sliced deli meat. Which gave her an idea.

"DONE!" COOKIE LOWERED the lid with a thud and dusted her hands off on her shorts. Then she exited the shed, turning off the light and latching the door shut behind her. When they'd bought the place it had come largely furnished already, which was a definite advantage for two women who had basically picked up and fled with only what they could carry. That had included the contents of the shed, which held a bunch of lawn chairs, a mower, a snowblower, and random gardening implements, as well as a large outdoor freezer. The kind where the lid lifted up to reveal nothing but a single big space that could easily fit a full-sized body. Or a few dozen kilos of illegal drugs.

They'd tossed a few emergency supplies in it, frozen peas, bottled water, and some meat, just on the off chance the fridge and freezer in the house died and they couldn't get food from the store for a few days. They hadn't opened the freezer since.

Until now. It was easy enough for Cookie to shove all the coke inside it and then heap the other contents on top to cover the drugs. She'd even been able to stow the now-empty lobster trap atop the freezer, which both kept all the evidence in one place and made it harder to get to the freezer itself.

As long as they didn't have a blackout coupled with a hurricane in the next few days, everything would be fine.

"Sweetie?" she heard Rain calling as she headed back around to the front porch.

"Here, Mom," Cookie shouted back, crossing the

threshold once more.

Rain stuck her head out from the kitchen. "Oh, there you are! I thought I heard you come back." A second later her mom emerged fully, wiping her hands on a dishtowel slung over her shoulder as she came down the hall. "How did it go?" Her eyes twinkled with mischief and the hope of good gossip. "Did you even get to the food?" Rain typically had only two things on her mind—getting high and getting laid. People who knew them already remarked how astounding it was that she and Cookie were even related, much less mother and daughter.

Of course, given that she was asking about what was supposed to have been a romantic picnic on a private island, for once Cookie could hardly blame her. She sighed. "Yes, we got to the food," she answered slowly, then frowned. She'd suddenly gotten a very clear image of the lobster roll Dylan had made sure she'd eaten. "Sort of."

"Sort of? What does that mean?" Rain demanded. "Either you were so distracted you didn't even remember to eat, or you ate first to make sure you had strength enough for dessert. Which was it?"

"It wasn't either." Cookie's locks were smooth in her hands as she grabbed her long hair and pulled it atop her head, twisting it into a messy bun just to have something to do. "We... found something out on the island. Something for the cops." She couldn't say what it was, of course. If Rain got even a hint that there was a whole mess of drugs hidden somewhere on their property, she'd tear the place apart looking for them. "We were so busy dealing with it we… kind of forgot to eat."

Her mother grinned and gave her daughter an exaggerated wink. "So you got right to it then. Good for you. I always knew you had it in you."

"Slow down, Blanche Devereaux. Nothing happened."

It took a second for Rain to process that, but when she did her smile vanished as suddenly as a rabbit down a hole. "Wait a second," she said, hands going to her hips. "Are you telling me that sexy-as-all-hell Dylan takes you all the way to this little island, just the two of you, with a gourmet lunch, oodles of privacy, and plenty of protection, and not only do you two not get busy but you don't even eat? Charlene Jamison, if I didn't have the stretch marks to prove it, I'd wonder if you were my child at all!"

"Tell me about it," Cookie muttered to herself. But her mother had a point, for a change. From a romantic standpoint, their lunch date had been a complete and utter flop. "We didn't mean for things to go the way they did," she explained, to herself as well as her mom. "And it started off really well. But then stuff happened, and, well—"

"Some crime or murder or something got in the way of you living an actual life," Rain finished for her. "I know. Seems like that's what always happens with you, doesn't it? Whether you want it to or not." She sounded unusually glum for a second, but then she shook her head, her spiky red-dyed hair swishing. "You didn't actually eat did you? How about Dylan?"

"I had a lobster roll. Dylan didn't get a chance."

Rain nodded. "Right. Call him."

"What?"

"You heard me. Call him," her mother repeated. "Tell him to meet you in the back down by the water in twenty minutes."

Cookie stared at her mother. "You want me to call Dylan and order him back here?" Her mother was grinning again, which was often a bad sign. "Mom, you do realize I'm not going to just throw myself at him when he gets here, right?"

"I know," Rain replied. "Shame, too—waste of a totally hot guy. But I know, morals, standards, public decency, yada, yada, yada. So we'll do it your way." She gave Cookie a wicked little smile. "Trust me, sweetie. I got this one." Then she sashayed back into the kitchen. Immediately the sound of pots and pans banging about filtered through the door...

I have absolutely no idea what she's got up her sleeve, Cookie admitted to herself, throwing up her hands. But while Rain could be totally out of control, and had no compunctions about breaking the law when it came to things like public nudity or recreational drug use, Cookie knew her mother did love her and worry about her. And Rain was really good with people, especially men. So if she had some sort of plan for how to salvage the day with

Dylan, Cookie was all ears.

I just hope, Cookie thought as she retrieved her phone and tapped out Dylan's number with her fingernail, that it really doesn't involve me stripping for him. Because that's not happening until at least the third date.

Or second at the absolute earliest—if they ever managed to complete one.

5.

"Hey," Dylan called out as he came around the side of the house at a brisk trot. "Everything okay?"

"Hmm?" Cookie had been staring out at the ocean. The sun was just starting to set, casting tracks of color across the water like a laser-light show from beneath the waves that lapped mesmerizingly against the dock, so it took her a second to focus on his question. "Sure, everything's fine." Then her brain caught up to her eyes, registering the concern on his face, and she smiled. "Yes, I'm good," she promised.

"Oh. Okay." She watched him visibly relax, though the slight scowl he'd been wearing morphed into a puzzled frown. "Sorry. It's just, when you called and told me to get my butt on over here—"

"I did not say that!" Cookie placed both hands on her hips and started at him, slightly perplexed. "I told you—no, I asked you to come out here and see me right away."

Dylan grinned at her. "Sure, sure. It's just that your questions sound an awful lot like commands." He raised an eyebrow. "Were you ever in the Army, by any chance? Drill sergeant, maybe?"

"Ha, ha." But she couldn't help smiling back. He seemed so amused and so pleased with himself. What was it about men? You could take the biggest, toughest, meanest of them and the second he cracked a dumb joke or made an awful pun, he reverted to being a little kid eager for approval. Not that she was complaining, especially since the goofy version of Dylan was pretty darn adorable, but it was one of those things she and Scarlett had pondered for many hours. Usually over stiff drinks.

Just then, the screened back door swung open with a squeak, and Rain stuck her head out. "Oh, hi, Dylan," she called out, waving. "Be right there!" Then she disappeared back inside.

Dylan glanced at Cookie, who shrugged. "No idea," she answered his unspoken question. "Easiest just to roll with it."

When Rain reappeared a minute later, she was carrying a large serving tray. Balancing it carefully, she made her way down the back steps and across the backyard toward them. Rain headed straight toward a small table that sat between two lounge chairs and set the platter down atop the table with a small sigh of relief. Then she straightened, tossed her head back, and smiled. "Dinner," she declared, "is served."

Curious, Cookie moved closer to investigate. They tray was packed with fruit salad, pasta salad, a plate of small sandwiches, another plate with cheese, crackers and sliced sausage, a bowl of olives, another bowl of hummus, and a third bowl with carrot sticks and celery stalks. There were also two beers, dripping condensation, and two bottles of water. "Mom, what is all this?" Cookie asked, completely stunned.

"Well, you said you and Dylan didn't really get to eat lunch, and I figured you must be hungry. So I threw together a few things for you." She waved at the food. "Sit. Eat. Enjoy." Then after giving Cookie a pointed look, she turned and beat a fast retreat for the house.

"Is this why you wanted me to come out here?" Dylan asked, startling her with his close proximity. He'd approached so quietly Cookie hadn't even heard him move, and now he slid past her to claim one of the lounge chairs. "Because it looks really good, and I am hungry."

"Yeah, me too." Cookie sank down onto the other lounge chair, shaking her head. Even after all these years, Rain was a mystery to her. Half the time the woman was the flightiest person on the planet, only thinking of herself and often barely thinking at all. Mostly she operated on pure instinct and a whole lot of lust. But then there were times like this when she opened up her heart, and she was the warmest, sweetest person in the world. The mom who would do anything, give up anything, take on anyone for her little girl. It was why, no matter what Rain did, no matter how irritating or embarrassing she got, Cookie was always able to look past it. Because she always knew, deep down, just how much her mother loved her.

For a few minutes the only sound was crunching as they ate, enjoying the food, the fine weather, the lovely twilight sky, and each other's company. But eventually, when a large portion of the meal had been demolished, they began talking again.

Dylan opened. "So," he asked slowly, glancing back behind him to make sure Rain wasn't listening in. "How did it go with the... ah, contraband?"

"Oh, good," Cookie answered quickly, keeping her voice low. "Safely tucked away, no worries. How about you?" Did she really just ask that? Now she felt like an idiot. "Not that you had anything to take care of," she corrected herself. "I'm the only one who would, right? Not that I would normally. I mean, this totally isn't my thing. But just this time, you know, under these circumstances, it was kind of all me, I guess. If that even makes any sense." She realized she was babbling and shut her mouth with a snap before she could say anything else even more foolish.

Dylan smiled, his dimples winking at her to match the twinkle in his blue eyes. "Something wrong?" he asked. He made a big show of looking around. "You seem a little nervous. Are you waiting for the next dead body or something?"

"What? No! Not at all. I mean, maybe, okay, it's best

to be prepared, sure, but I'm not expecting anything, if that's what you mean. I don't have one on order." *You're doing it again*, she warned herself, winding down with a muttered, "That would be weird."

Dylan was openly laughing at her now. "Weird does seem to be your speed," he pointed out. "Also dangerous, risky, and deadly." He shook his head as he reached for his beer. "You and your simple life, I guess."

She wanted to deny that charge, but knew she couldn't, so she snatched up her own beer bottle instead. It was cold in her palms as she rolled it back and forth between both hands. "I can't help it," she said finally, eyes on the bottle instead of the man across from her. "I don't mean for these things to find me, but somehow they do." She shuddered. "It's like I'm a crime magnet or something."

"You don't have to be." She could tell from his voice that he was being serious again, and she glanced up at him through her hair, which had come loose and was hanging over her face as she leaned forward. Sure enough, the dimples had fled as he said, "Hand the drugs over to Swan. Or, if you don't trust him, directly to Watkins. Give them to the cops and let them handle it. It's not your problem. Not unless you insist on making it yours."

Cookie knew he was right. They'd stumbled upon the lobster trap. That hadn't been her fault, but instead of bringing the trap and its contents to the authorities, Cookie had opted to bring them home with her instead.

That wasn't just foolish, it was potentially criminal if her actions impeded their eventual investigation. That could be a problem if the sheriff or deputy ever looked into the matter. If, on the other hand, Deputy Swan just let it drop as he'd done in the past with other investigations, then Cookie was the only one willing to figure out exactly what was going on and how to stop it.

So apparently Dylan was right. When faced with the choice to cast it all aside and trust others to handle the investigation despite her claims of wanting a simple life, Cookie didn't hesitate even for a second.

It was full speed ahead.

Still, she wasn't quite ready to consider that a bad thing, not yet. "Okay, so I don't turn my back on cases when they fall in my lap. But that's a good thing. Especially considering all that's happened here. You can't drop me at ground zero and then accuse me of starting the fireworks."

"You're right," Dylan agreed. "You didn't cause all this to happen. But you've been here for all of it. That sure doesn't feel like a coincidence." He shook his head. "Whether you're somehow a magnet for this or just unlucky, I've got no idea. You have to admit that you like it, though. You're drawn to the danger, and the craziness. Tell me I'm wrong."

She met his eyes, which had darkened to flint, and couldn't say anything.

"Right." He sighed deeply. "So what happens when the excitement ends? When the crime stops? Because before you moved here, it was nice and quiet. Peaceful. Safe. So what are you going to do when all that comes back? When there isn't anything dangerous to hold your interest?"

With a sudden flash, Cookie understood what Dylan was asking and why. "I'm not going anywhere," she vowed, leaning in toward him to catch a whiff of woodsy-scented soap. "I promise."

He started to respond, the look on his face suggesting that he planned to argue. But then Cookie suddenly lunged forward, barely avoiding the tray, and kissed him, her lips slamming into his with enough force to push him backward.

Dylan recovered and held strong, the contents of the tray clamoring as he shoved it aside and reached for Cookie, his arms wrapping around her waist and pulling her in close. The awkwardness slipped away, their lips soft and supple as they nibbled at each other like the perfect dessert to their makeshift picnic. *Dylan.* She was *kissing* Dylan. And it was amazing.

Cookie wasn't inexperienced at the ol' lip-lock. She'd kissed guys with firm lips, soft lips, scratchy lips, thin lips, thick lips, all sorts. But she honestly couldn't remember a kiss as good as this.

Part of that was because right now she couldn't remember much of anything. Hell, she wasn't one hundred percent sure of her own name at the moment. The embrace was taking away her ability to think or move or do much of anything else. Which only proved how good it was. Because although she'd heard about people being kissed senseless, this was certainly the first time she'd ever experienced it herself. So she silenced her inner dialogue and stopped trying to think, at least for a little while. All she wanted right then was Dylan.

Eventually their lips parted, and both of them pulled back a little. Not far, but just enough so that they could breathe, and also meet each other's eyes. His had shifted to a bright, clear, almost sapphire blue, Cookie noted.

"Wow," he said after a second. He chest heaved from breathing heavily, like he'd just run a marathon, and his face was flushed.

"Yeah," she agreed. She was gasping a bit as well.

"So does that mean you like me?" he asked, an impish smile twitching at his lips and matching the light in his crinkling eyes. "Or were you just demonstrating how much all this danger and weirdness turns you on?"

"Shut up," Cookie warned, slapping him lightly on the chest. But she was already leaning in. Then they were kissing again, and she hoped he'd forgotten his questions, because she certainly had.

This time they parted more quickly, which was disappointing. Still reeling from the kiss, she frowned as she tried to focus, to figure out why her lips were separated from Dylan's. But she could hardly think straight with all the commotion coming from the inn.

Wait, what?

Cooking turned and stared toward the house, fully registering the fact that Rain was screaming her name.

Dylan, already looking in that direction, cleared his throat, and in an oddly flat, even cold voice, said, "Looks like your mom wants to give us a hand."

Cookie's heart lurched as her gaze landed on her frantic mother and the severed body part she was holding.

6.

"COOKIE! COOKIEEEEEEEE!!!" RAIN ran across the backyard, waving her hands—all three of them—at Cookie and Dylan.

Leaping to her feet, Cookie staggered into motion, meeting Rain halfway. "It's okay, Mom," she promised, reaching out to capture her mother's wrists as gently as she could. And now, with her mother finally stilled, Cookie was able to confirm what she'd seen and not quite believed before.

Rain was clutching an extra hand.

"Dylan, grab me a napkin or something," Cookie called out. A second later he was beside her, one of the inn's cloth napkins held out like an offering. She took it, draped it over her fingers and thumb, and used it to pry the unfamiliar limb from her mother's panicked death grip. Then, taking a step back, Cookie examined the appendage.

It was a man's hand, she saw at once. Long, thick fingers, heavy, swollen joints, coarse reddish-brown hair coating the back, thick calluses lining the ridge just below the fingers in front. The odor of death told her it was real, right down to the jagged edge where the flesh had been cut away at the wrist, and the sawed-off bone. There wasn't any blood, or at least nothing dripped down on her, so it had had time to coagulate, and the fingers were stiff when she pushed at them. Rigor mortis had definitely set in and not yet faded, which could yield an approximate time of death. She held it up against her own hand to get a sense of scale. Whoever the hand had come from, he was probably at least her height, maybe taller, and—

A rasping sound came from behind her, interrupting her train of thought. Cookie turned to find Dylan standing there, arms crossed, shaking his head. "I need a plastic bag," she told him, brandishing the hand in his direction.

"Sure." He didn't seem freaked out by the severed limb, but he didn't look all that eager to take it from her, either. Instead he edged around her and headed toward the house and the kitchen. With him gone, Cookie turned to her mother.

Rain hadn't budged since surrendering the hand. She was still standing there, eyes wide, face pale, wringing her own hands together. "Mom," Cookie said to her, then tried again, louder, when Rain didn't respond. "Mom!"

That made Rain's head snap in her direction, and after a second her mother drew a deep, shuddering breath, her eyes finally focusing on Cookie's face.

"Mom, where did this come from?" Cookie asked softly. "Did you find it somewhere, or did someone give it to you?"

Her mother snorted, showing a grain of her usual spark. "Even if I'd found a hand lying about somewhere, do you really think I'd pick it up and bring it home?" She shook her head. "That's more your thing, dear."

"Body parts? I don't think so mother," Cookie shot back, mildly insulted.

"Well, you were always bringing me birds with broken wings, abandoned and possibly abused cats and dogs, and even that turtle with a hurt leg. For goodness sake, there were so many, I just knew you were going to be a vet. You definitely missed your calling, dear."

Cookie clamped her mouth shut to keep from correcting her mother over the decade-old argument. Now wasn't the time. Rain had understood that her daughter had sympathized with damaged animals, of course. But beyond that, Cookie had burned with fury at whomever had hurt them, and with the fierce desire to make it right somehow. That's why she'd gone for punishing criminals instead of bandaging hurt paws. She'd rather get justice than soothe pain any day.

"So if you didn't find the hand, where did you get it?" Cookie asked again. Dylan had reemerged from the inn, holding a large sealable freezer bag. Perfect.

"Thanks," she told him as the bag rustled when he opened it and held it out so she could deposit the hand inside. "Mom?"

"Hmm?" Rain was frowning at the bagged hand like it was somehow to blame, and Cookie wondered if her mother was in shock. "Oh. You got a package."

"I got a package?" Cookie stared at her. "When? Where? What does that have to do with anything?"

Her mother sighed. "It was right after I brought out your dinner." She took a second to shoot an accusing glare at the overturned tray and the remains of the picnic scattered about on the ground. "Somebody knocked, and it was a courier." A slow, predatory smile spread across her face. "Cute, too. Very cute." Apparently shock wasn't the problem here. "About six feet tall, slim but not too skinny. You know how I don't like them bony. What's the point if there isn't at least a little meat to grab, right? Dark, curly hair, a little long. Nice nose, not too big but not a little button either. I've never liked those. They're fine on lap dogs but men? No way. Brown eyes, very warm. Good smile, chipped front tooth but still open and friendly. He had—"

"Mom!" On the one hand, Cookie was glad that her mother seemed to be fine. On the other, she really didn't need a detailed description of some random delivery guy right now, especially since she knew her mother's recounting was probably about to head south—in more ways than one. "So this guy showed up with a package for me. What then?"

"Oh, well, we chatted a minute. But he said he had other deliveries to make, so he left, though I think he wanted to ask for my number. So hopefully he—" At another glare from Cookie, Rain visibly shook herself. "Right. So you had this package, and it didn't have a return address. I thought that was weird, but didn't think much of it. Small town and all. And you and Dylan were having such a nice time out here." She paused long enough to smirk at them, which made Cookie's face heat up. "So I figured I'd just go ahead and open the package for you, so as not to disturb your dinner."

Cookie groaned. "Mom, you do know that messing with someone else's mail is a federal offense, right?"

But Rain just waved that off. "Oh, phooie! I'm not messing, I'm your mother."

Cookie decided to ignore that, though she noticed Dylan was trying hard not to laugh. "So you opened this package that had been addressed to me. And?"

"And I noticed right away that it smelled funny," Rain answered. She paused then gave Cookie a self-satisfied smile. "Yes, that's right, it smelled funny. That's why I opened it. I was worried that whatever was in it might be spoiled or something, so I thought I'd better take care of it right away, before it got worse."

"Of course you did." Cookie didn't have the heart to point out that Rain had just completely contradicted herself. It just wasn't worth the effort.

"And when I opened the box, there it was." Rain grimaced as she pointed at the severed hand. "It was horrible! So I grabbed it and ran to get you."

Thereby destroying a ton of potential evidence, Cookie thought, biting back a groan. Fingerprints, tape, fibers,

DNA, etc. Who knew how much Rain had obliterated out of curiosity and then panic? "Was there anything else in the box?" she asked, forcing her voice to remain calm.

Her mother frowned. "I don't know," she admitted, her brow creasing in concentration. "I can't remember. Maybe? Yes! Yes, I think there was. A piece of paper. Like a note or a card." She turned back toward the house. "I'll go get it."

"No!" Cookie caught herself after her mother recoiled from the shout and continued in a more normal tone. "I'll get it. Thanks. I'll be right back."

"Oh. All right." Her mother looked a little hurt. "I'll just pick up the dinner I made for you, then."

"It was really good, Mom," Cookie managed, and was pleased to see her mother brighten a little. "Really. And incredibly sweet of you. Thank you."

As Cookie trudged toward the house, plastic bag still firmly in her grasp, she heard Dylan compliment Rain on dinner, as well. She made a mental note to thank him later. He'd totally charm Rain out of her funk, which left Cookie to focus on this package and its meaning.

She found the box easily enough. It was sitting on the little table just inside the front door, the one where they placed their mail and their keys and the sign-in book for guests. It was a standard cardboard container, and her name and "Secret Seal Inn" were written on it in what looked like black marker. She winced at how the box had been torn open, as well as the rank odor, then used a pen to push back the flaps and peer inside.

Sure enough, a folded piece of paper lay within.

Cookie still had the napkin Dylan had handed her, and used it to carefully collect the note. The thick cloth of the napkin made fine motor control a lot harder. Crushing the note or ruining any trace it might carry would be detrimental to the investigation. But finally she managed to extract the letter from the box and lay it out on the table.

It was a short note, and straight to the point:

You have something of ours. Tell no one. We'll be in touch.

That was it. Cookie had no doubt what "something" they were referring to. The question was who were "they," and how had they known she'd taken the drugs?

"That can't be good," a voice commented from behind her. Cookie whirled about, dropping reflexively into a defensive pose at the same time she reached for her gun, the metal warm on her fingers. "Whoa," Dylan said, holding up both hands and backing away a step. "Sorry. Should've let you know I was here, huh?"

"Yeah," Cookie agreed, wondering once again where he'd learned to move so silently. "And no, it's not good." She glanced past Dylan, toward the kitchen. "Where's mom?"

"She's busy putting stuff away," he assured her, keeping his voice low so it wouldn't carry. He gestured with his chin toward the note. "I'm assuming they're talking about that thing from earlier?"

"Has to be," she agreed. "And this"—she waved the hand in its bag—"is their idea of a warning."

"Pretty nasty warning." He shook his head. "What were you saying about a simple life, and the quiet, and so on?"

"I didn't ask for this," she pointed out. "You were there, you saw. We just stumbled onto it and into whatever all this is."

But Dylan wasn't arguing. Instead he was staring at the note. Finally, he sighed. "I guess this means you're calling Hunter," he said. His whole body was tense, as if he was prepared for a fight.

Cookie understood. He and Hunter had gotten off on the wrong foot right from the start, with Hunter acting the possessive partner and then interrogating Dylan about Chip's murder. Things hadn't exactly improved from there. True, they'd managed to put their differences aside a few times when Dylan had helped them go after Stone Harris, and again when Hayley had been blackmailed. But both men were strong, stubborn, used to being in charge, and evidently interested in her. And neither was willing to share.

Still, at least Dylan understood that this was the sort of thing that really needed Hunter's attention. It wasn't personal. So she shrugged and said, "Yeah, I think he needs to know about this." She didn't bother to mention that she'd already talked to him, and that he was already on his way. There was nothing to gain from elaborating.

Dylan nodded. "I'd better get going," he said,

turning toward the front door. He stopped mid-motion, however, to eye her seriously. "You okay?"

"I'm fine," she assured him. "But thanks." She hoped that her warm tone was enough to convey how much she meant that. She wasn't one of those women who got offended when a man tried to help her. She would get mighty pissed if he insisted on helping after she'd made it clear she neither needed nor wanted help. But checking on her after someone delivered a nasty threat along with a severed hand? Definitely not going to get up in arms about that one.

She thought he understood, because he smiled as he left. Still, she couldn't help but notice that he hadn't tried to kiss her goodnight. Then again, she was still holding the severed hand and a loaded gun. A lot of guys would probably consider that a mood-killer.

Cookie hoped that was all it wound up killing.

7.

COOKIE WAS STILL standing in the front hall, the severed limb in one hand and the note in her other, when Rain finally emerged from the kitchen.

"What are you going to do with that...thing?" her mother asked hesitantly, very unlike her usual boisterous self. But at least she seemed composed, Cookie thought. Composed...and maybe a little glassy-eyed. Still, if toking up was what it took for her to get past the shock she'd just experienced, Cookie was hardly going to begrudge her.

Truth be told, she didn't have a problem with people getting high as long as it didn't ruin their lives or put anyone else at risk. She did think that Rain took it a bit too far sometimes. If her mother got in trouble with the law, Cookie could probably get her cleared without too much trouble, but that kind of attention could expose them both. It wasn't something either of them needed. But deep down, Cookie had to admit that her mother's personality was just as much a risk as her penchant for the Mary Jane. The woman made a big deal out of everything. There was just as much a chance she'd do something crazy that would expose them as there was of her getting into trouble with the law over a minor drug infraction.

Still, Rain had raised Cookie singlehandedly, working a variety of jobs to keep a roof over both their heads, food on the table, and money for textbooks and whatever else they needed, so clearly she was no stranger to responsibility. Because of that, Cookie cut her mother a lot of slack.

Right now, for example, Rain was certainly lucid enough to be asking an important question. And Cookie felt that deserved a proper answer. "It's evidence of a crime, maybe more than one, so I really should turn it over to the proper authorities. The only problem with that is—"

"Deputy Swan is a big fat butthead," her mother finished for her.

Cookie had to laugh at that. "Yeah, that about sums it up," she agreed.

Just like Dylan and Hunter hadn't gotten along from the get-go, she and Swan had started on the absolute wrong foot. And maybe part of that was her fault, both for not revealing her FBI background and for taking offense easily. But when a dead body washes up on your property and you report it, you don't expect the local law to pat you on the head and say, "Oh, don't worry your pretty little head about it." Which was basically what

Swan had done.

If he'd had his way, there never would have been an investigation at all. And sure, Stone Harris hadn't meant for Chip Winslow to die, but still even a slug like him deserved some justice. Or at least closure.

But Swan couldn't be bothered. With that, or much of anything else. He'd told Cookie once that he liked being the only deputy on the island because it was quiet and nobody expected much of him except to break up the occasional barroom brawl or to rescue the rare treed cat. Nothing much ever happened here, so he could just sit back in his office and play on his computer all day.

Except, as Dylan had pointed out, since Cookie's arrival they'd had two deaths, one blackmailing, and now one major drug score. Plus one severed hand. Not exactly the quiet Swan enjoyed so much.

Cookie knew she had to call him. If she had any respect for the badge and the office, which she did, just not the man holding them, she needed to report it properly. But she still couldn't forgive him for accidentally misplacing a piece of crucial evidence in the Dickie Dungworth case. And she was giving him the benefit of the doubt by believing his claim that it had even been an accident. So how was she supposed to trust him with this?

And while she could just go over his head and call Sheriff Watkins directly, again, that was disrespectful. While the FBI wasn't exactly the military, they did share the same respect for the chain of command. Swan was

Watkins's representative here. He was the one she needed to call. Cookie sighed. Better to get it over with.

"So you're going to call him after all?" Rain asked as Cookie set the hand down on the table with a soft thud and picked up the phone.

"I have to," Cookie replied, punching in the number she'd already memorized. "It's the right thing to do."

Much to her surprise, Rain nodded. "If it means getting that thing out of here," she stated, gesturing at the bagged limb, "I'm all for it." Which only emphasized how upset she was, because normally Rain hated having anything to do with the cops, inept or otherwise.

The call connected, sparing Cookie from having to reply. "Secret Seal Sheriff's Office," a soft male voice answered. "Whatd'ya need?"

Cookie frowned. "Deputy Swan?" His words were too mealy, too run together. Too...slurred.

"That's right," he said. "I'm Deputy Swan. I'm the law around these parts. Who is this, and what do you want?"

Oh, he was definitely drunk. *Very* drunk. Cookie reflexively checked her watch. It was just past eight o'clock. Clearly Swan had started early.

"It's Cookie James," she said, bulling ahead. She did her best to ignore the groan he made. "You remember that matter I called you about earlier?" Rain was standing nearby, making it impossible for her elaborate about the drugs. Cookie hated herself for thinking the worst of her own mother, but she was honest enough to admit that it wasn't worth taking the risk. "Well, there's been a new development."

"What matter? Talk plain sense, woman!" Swan barked over the phone. "What now? You find another body? How is it you're always finding bodies? I've been here two years, I never once found a body. Not that I want to, mind you. But you're here a couple a' days and you've tripping over bodies left and right."

Cookie tightened her grip on the receiver, trying to do the same with her rapidly fraying temper. "We've been here over a month now, Deputy," she reminded him, not bothering to soften her tone. "But yes, you are correct, I have found a couple bodies in that time. I don't know why." She shrugged, even though she knew the gesture was lost on him. "Just lucky, I guess."

He snorted. "Lucky? Woman, if you were stumbling on gold bricks or wads of cash, I'd agree. But stiffs? How's that lucky? That's just morbid—and weird."

A small part of her was impressed that he could remember the word morbid, much less use it correctly in his current state. "Well, setting aside our varying definitions of luck," she said, "I've got another one." She eyed the hand. "Or at least part of one."

"What, a body?"

"Yes, part of a body. A hand, to be specific. Someone mailed it to me."

She could practically hear his jaw drop. And she definitely heard him sputter before he spoke clearly. "Someone mailed you a hand?"

"Yes."

"Did they put the stamps right on it, or did they wrap it in bubble-tape first?" And then he giggled like a twelve-year-old girl. When did a grown man giggle anymore? Especially over something as grisly as a hand. Apparently when he was stinkin' drunk.

"It was in a box," Cookie told him, rolling her eyes at her mother, who nodded. Good to know that Deputy Swan was singlehandedly reinforcing all of Rain's prejudices against cops. "With a note."

"Was it a ransom note? Give me the drugs or I send you another body part?" He was still giggling, but a little less now. Hopefully the idea of someone slicing pieces off a person was sobering him up some, but Cookie wasn't counting on it.

"Not exactly. But close." She sighed, and the cramping in her hand forced her to open her fingers one at a time before resettling them in a gentler hold on the phone. "Can I bring them by?"

That made him stop chuckling, at least. "You want to bring the hand *here*? To my office?"

"Well, you are the deputy," she reminded him. "You're 'the law around these parts.' Isn't that what you said?"

"Sure, sure, but I don't want some dead hand stinking up the place!" There was a loud clattering on the other end of the line, and Cookie suspected Swan had been leaning back with his feet up and had only now shifted to a normal sitting position. Judging by the noise, he had nearly toppled over as a result. Which was all she needed, she thought, for him to fall over and break his neck while talking to her. How would that look? What would Dylan say about that one? That now she was actually causing dead bodies, and over the phone, nonetheless? She'd need to wear a sign on her forehead that read, *Caution, do not approach, may cause sudden death.* Which would pretty much rule out any more kissing.

She forced herself back to the topic at hand. "Okay, so you don't want me to bring you this hand?" she asked slowly, just to make sure they were all clear.

"No," Swan answered at once. "No, I do not. You can keep it."

Do not kill him, she reminded herself. *Not even if you want to.* "It is evidence of a crime, you know. And you are the deputy."

"I don't want a hand!" he yelled in her ear. "Somebody sent it to you. You deal with it."

"So you're saying you want me to take this case?" Cookie asked. She shifted around in an attempt ignore her mother, who was frantically shaking her head no. "And that I shouldn't bother you with it anymore?"

"Yes!" She had to hold the phone away from her ear to keep from being deafened. "Yes, you take it! You took the other two. You can take this one, too. Talk to the sheriff. Just don't bring it round here, got it?" A clattering sounded over the line as he hung up on her.

Cookie waited another second, just in case the line reactivated, then slowly set the receiver back on its hook.

"Oh," Rain said with a sigh. "Oh, dear. Why'd you do that, sweetie? Now we're stuck with that horrible thing."

"I know, Mom." Cookie nodded. "Sorry about that. Believe me, I don't want it around here any more than you do. But Deputy Swan was pretty clear about it."

"That man," her mother declared, "is a bumbling idiot!"

"He sure is," Cookie agreed. But deep down she was actually pleased with how that conversation had gone. Because, if she were being honest with herself, she'd hated the idea of handing this case over to Swan, even if it was only until Hunter could get out here. Now she didn't have to, because with the deputy's blessing, the case was hers. And she hadn't even asked for it, so no one could accuse her of stepping on Swan's toes.

Of course, that still left her with a severed hand. It was too late to do anything with it tonight, so she'd have to deal with it in the morning. Which meant she'd have to stow it someplace safe for now. Fortunately, she knew exactly the place. And if she'd thought that Rain wouldn't find the drugs before, she knew they'd be safe from her now. With a severed hand sitting on top of them, her mother wouldn't go near that freezer even if her life depended upon it.

Scooping up the hand, Cookie headed for the front door. "I'm going to go store this," she called out as she left. "I'll be right back. Don't touch anything, okay?"

For once, she suspected her mother would actually do exactly as she was told.

8.

THE NEXT MORNING, the shrill ring of Cookie's phone woke her from a sound sleep. Groggily she grabbed for it, but it clattered on the floor when she managed to knock it off the bedside table. She lunged out of bed, scrambled around for it on the cold, hard wood, and then found it tucked into one of her shoes. Out of breath, with her heart pounding, she flopped back on the bed and answered the call.

"This had better be the most amazing thing ever," she declared into the phone, leaning back against her pillow and shoving her hair out of her face.

"Well, not to toot my own horn," a deep, sexy male voice replied, "but I *am* pretty great. Or so I've been told."

"Hunter!" Sitting up, Cookie glared at the bedside clock. It claimed that it was already 6:59 in the morning, and even as she watched the numbers shift to 7:00, she took that as a personal betrayal. "Are you here? Tell me you're here. You're not, though, right? Because it's early.

Too early. Why are you calling this early if you're not here?"

Her former partner's warm chuckle sounded in her ear. "And a good morning to you too," he said. "Nice to see you're still just as out of it when you wake up." That brought a flush to her face and chest, even though the closest Hunter had ever been to seeing her when she woke up was the time she'd fallen asleep while they were on a stakeout. "No, I'm not there yet. About to board, actually. Should be there sometime tonight. I think they're saying around six."

"Oh. Okay. Great." Not for the first time, Cookie cursed how far Secret Seal Isle was from anything resembling a big city—or a major airport—and how long and tedious it was to get out here. Then again, that had been the point. It was just damned inconvenient at times like this. "Call me when you're on the ferry, and I'll meet you at the dock."

"Will do." He got serious, then. "Everything okay? Any new developments?"

"Yeah, you could say that." Sitting there cross-legged on her bed in sleep shorts and an oversized T-shirt, she proceeded to tell him about the ghastly package she'd received and Rain's reaction when she'd foolishly opened it.

"Serves her right," Hunter decided after she'd finished. "Still, that's pretty high on the creep factor."

"I know, right?" Cookie turned toward her windows, where even through the curtains the glare of the sunlight made her squint. Was everything against her this morning? "And you'll be proud of me. For once I didn't try to Lone Wolf it." She recounted her call to Deputy Swan.

"Wow." This time Hunter's voice was low and flat, a clear sign of his disapproval. "I didn't see that one coming. I mean, the man's useless, but getting drunk on the job? That's pathetic."

"Yeah, well, I guess it doesn't help that I keep showing him up," Cookie admitted. Not that she felt a lot of sympathy for Swan. "Anyway, I was going to take the hand over to Jared this morning and get him to start running tests, see what he can find out."

"Good idea. Maybe he'll have something by the time I get in."

"That's what I'm going for." She smiled. "See you later?"

"You know it." He hung up, and Cookie sat there for a minute, staring at the phone in her hand. Damn. She'd always thought it was unfair that her partner was so hot. Life would've been a lot easier if she'd shared her cases with a fat, frumpy, middle-aged married guy. Not as interesting, probably, but a lot easier.

Still, the partner she did have was on his way out here, which meant she'd better get moving. With a groan and one last accusing stare at the alarm clock, Cookie hopped out of bed. Stretching and yawning, she trekked toward the bathroom at the end of the hall. She already had the feeling this was going to be a long day.

Cookie's mood improved slightly after a hot shower and clean clothes, and she traipsed downstairs and into the kitchen.

"Morning, sweetie!" Rain called cheerfully as the aroma of coffee wafted toward Cookie. "Good timing. I just finished making breakfast." Rain appeared as if she'd been up for hours, which might have been the case. She'd always been an early riser, and had usually finished her yoga long before Cookie could drag herself out of bed. The good news was, that meant Rain usually had breakfast ready and waiting for her. And today was no exception. There were eggs and bacon, hash browns, toast, orange juice and, of course, a fresh pot of coffee that tantalized Cookie's need to wake up. She reached for the coffee first, taking a long drink from her mug.

"Mom, you're a godsend," she told Rain as she dished some food onto her plate. Since their last guest had left the morning before, the two of them ate in the kitchen where it was nice and cozy and meant one less room to clean when they were done.

"Thanks." Her mother beamed at the compliment. Her chair creaked when she sat down and took some food for herself. "So," she said after they'd both had a chance to eat a bit, "what's the plan for today?"

"I'm taking the hand over to Hancock," Cookie answered after a big bite of toast piled high with eggs, bacon, and hash browns. Hey, she could multi-task. "I'm going to give it to the medical examiner there, Jared. See what he can tell me."

"Ooh, sounds exciting," Rain said, setting down her fork and looking at Cookie with big eyes. "A medical examiner? Is that like a doctor? I've been medically examined plenty of times." She giggled at her own joke.

"What? No! Ew." Cookie waved that image away as best she could.

"I could use another check-up," Rain said, leaning in conspiratorially.

"Oh no," Cookie said quickly, understanding exactly what her mother was suggesting. "No way. Definitely not. Uh-uh."

"But why not?" Rain whined, gazing at her daughter with sad puppy dog eyes. "I never get to see what you do when you're on a case. It'd be exciting." She sighed and glanced down at her hands. "Besides, I—I'm a little scared to be here all alone right now. What if whoever sent you that...you know, comes back looking for it? Or for you?"

Cookie started to tell Rain she was being ridiculous, but then stopped herself. Okay, sure, her mother was being melodramatic, as always, but she did have a point. Whoever had sent that package had known where Cookie lived. What if they did come back while Rain was here by herself? For now, until she figured out more—and until Hunter arrived—it might be a good idea to keep her mother close. Which is why, much to her own horror, Cookie found herself saying, "Okay, fine. You can come along."

"Really?" Rain practically squealed with delight. "Oh,

thank you, sweetie. This is going to be so much fun!" Her plate clattered in the sink where she dumped it, and she bustled out, presumably to go get ready.

Yeah, fun, Cookie thought as she watched Rain leave. *My mother doing a ride-along on a case involving drugs and severed limbs. Should be an absolute blast.*

9.

LATER THAT MORNING, Cookie led her mother into the Hancock sheriff's station. "Jared's down in the basement," she explained as they headed for the stairs. "That's where the morgue usually is."

"The morgue?" Rain stared at her, horrified. "You didn't say anything about a morgue. Will there be dead bodies everywhere?"

"They don't keep them just out in the open, no," Cookie replied. She was already regretting this decision, and had been ever since she'd agreed to it. Rain's enthusiasm had worn on her the whole way into town. It was like dealing with an energetic small child who sucked all the energy right out of you until all you wanted to do was faceplant. "It's fine," she said as much to reassure herself as to console her mother.

When they reached the morgue and pushed the doors open, Rain breathed a loud, dramatic sigh of relief. There weren't any bodies out at all, and the only person in the room was one Jared Delgado, Hancock Medical

Examiner. He'd discarded his shoes and had his feet up on one of the exam tables, kicked back as he watched something on the computer screen across from him. Obviously it was another busy day here in the heart of the crime wave that was coastal Maine.

"Hey, Jared," Cookie called out as they entered. That got an immediate, and very amusing response. Jared jerked upright and yanked back his feet like they were on fire, swiveling and planting both feet on the ground. He yelped as the cold tile of the floor touched his socks, making him cringe, but he tried to cover that by puffing out his chest.

Ah, men.

"Hello, Cookie!" Jared shouted back before remembering himself and lowering his volume. "Always a delight to see you. And who might this vision of loveliness be?" He gestured at Rain, who simpered like a little girl.

"This is my mother, Rain," Cookie said. "Rain, this is Doctor Jared Delgado, the county's chief medical examiner."

Jared stepped forward, still twitching a little each time his feet touched the cold floor. Being the morgue, the room was kept almost as cold as an icebox. "Charmed, Madame," he told Rain when he reached them. Taking her hand in his, he swept into a deep bow. "It is rare to find so much beauty in such a dark, bleak place as this."

Rain tittered a bit more. Jared grinned at Cookie like

he was a dog who'd just done something clever and now expected a treat. Unfortunately for him, Cookie only gave him a flat stare. "That's swell, Jared, but can we put the poetry on hold for a minute?"

His smile slid away, and his expression transformed into one of a wounded puppy.

"Oh, Cookie, be nice," Rain reprimanded. "I think he's sweet." She smiled at Jared, batting her lashes, and the poor man blushed. It was obvious he didn't get a lot of female attention, but right then was not the time.

"I need to know what you can tell me about this," Cookie said, pulling the bag out of her purse and holding it up between them. Most people might have recoiled at having a severed hand thrust in their face, even one safely ensconced in a plastic bag. But Jared was hardly most people.

"You do bring the most interesting things," he murmured, reaching out to take the bag from her. "Where did you get this? Was someone getting too handsy with you?" He chuckled at his own pun, and Rain giggled. Cookie rolled her eyes.

"Someone mailed it to me," she answered. "In a box. With a warning."

"Some warning," the medical examiner commented, carrying the hand back over to his desk and sitting down so he could study it under the light. "It's a man's, obviously. Adult, mature, but not old. Caucasian, red-brown hair. It appears weathered, so it most likely belongs to someone who works outside or at least is outside a lot." After pulling on a pair of gloves, he extracted the hand from its bag and examined it more closely. "I'll want to run some tests, but it looks like it was removed post-mortem. Not by much, though."

Cookie nodded then turned to Rain, who had been listening, but judging by the perplexed look on her face, she wasn't following. "Whoever's hand this is," she explained to her mother, "was dead when they cut it off. But he hadn't been that way for long."

Rain turned pale. "So they killed him and then cut off his hand?"

"Probably, yeah." Cookie frowned. "Which means we've got another murder to investigate."

She could only guess what Dylan would have to say about that.

"What about IDing the vic?" Cookie asked. "Any hope of pulling his fingerprints?"

"Hmm, unlikely," Jared beckoned her over.

Rain shrank back, but Cookie didn't. She'd seen dead bodies before, and things way more grisly than an unattached hand. Sidling up beside Jared, she did her best to ignore him glancing surreptitiously up at her chest. She didn't want to embarrass the poor guy. One cheap thrill for the lab geek wouldn't hurt anything, right?

Jared pulled the adjustable arm of the magnifying lens across the table and positioned it over the hand's forefinger and thumb. "Take a look."

Cookie leaned in, squinting. "Something's wrong

with the prints," she said after a second. Water damage was one thing, but the hand didn't look particularly wrinkly, nor did it have that loose, saggy look of flesh that had been soaking for too long. But where the fingerprints should have been, there was only the faintest remains of the identifying lines. "Deliberate, you think?"

"Almost certainly," the medical examiner replied, his face turning bright red as he tried turning toward her and nearly got a face-full of boob. "I'll run some tests, though. I might still be able to get something. DNA for sure, but sometimes it's possible to reconstruct fingerprints."

"Great. Let me know what you find." She squeezed his shoulder and noticed the muscle harden as he flexed for her. "Thanks, Jared. You're the best."

That made him blush even more. "Happy to help," he managed to stammer out.

"Come on, Mom, let's go," Cookie said, and Rain nodded.

"It was so nice meeting you," Rain gushed at Jared, who had regained enough composure to smile back at her.

"An absolute pleasure, Mrs. James," he assured her.

"Oh, it's Miss Forest," Rain was quick to point out, waggling the fingers of her left hand so he could see the lack of a ring. "I'm one-hundred-percent available. And *you* can call me Rain."

Cookie latched an arm through her mother's and dragged her out before she could put any more moves on the hapless ME.

"He's a cutie," Rain stage-whispered as the morgue doors swung shut behind them. "A little nerdy, but sweet. And I bet he'd appreciate a real woman."

"He's less than half your age, Mom," Cookie pointed out as their feet pounded when they climbed the stairs. "And he works with dead bodies all day. Imagine the small talk you'd get from that." She had nothing against Jared, actually, but she didn't want to see him get sucked into her mother's web. That way lay madness. And since she might have to work with him again, if there was any fallout from a failed romance with Rain, she'd be the one bearing the brunt of it. Better to nip any ideas in the bud now, while she still could.

"You never let me have any fun," Rain claimed, sticking out her lower lip just like a petulant toddler.

"Hey, I let you come to a sheriff's station with me. Isn't this fun?" Cookie replied as they reached the main level of the building. "If you behave, I'll see if I can get you a toy badge." Just then she spotted Sheriff Watkins through the glass. "Hang on, I need to talk to someone while we're here."

"What, in there?" Rain shrank back, a look of defiance on her face as Cookie steered them toward the rest of the office. "Maybe I should wait outside."

Cookie didn't have the patience for her mother's nonsense. "You're straight and sober right now, right?" she demanded. Her mother could only nod. "Then you're fine. Just keep your mouth shut and we'll be in and out in no time." She pushed the heavy door open and led the way.

The Hancock sheriff's office wasn't exactly huge, and there were only a few people on staff, so it was no surprise that the sheriff noticed them right away. She smiled and headed toward them, intersecting their path right by the front desk.

"Cookie, hello!" As always, Sheriff Watkins reminded her of somebody's grandma—short, stout, graying, and smiling, but with that hint of sternness behind it that invariably kept you inline. "I wasn't expecting you, was I?" Then she turned toward Rain and offered her hand. "Hello, I'm Sheriff Watkins, nice to meet you."

"This is my mother, Rain Forest," Cookie explained, wincing like she did every time she had to use her mother's full name. Well, current full name. Her real name was Mary Arlene Jamison. Her mother had argued that if they were going into hiding she wanted a name that represented her inner spirit, whatever that meant. Cookie had been in no position to disagree seeing as how she'd gone from Charlene Jamison to Cookie James herself. But her mother, being her mother, had to take it ten steps further. Rather than choosing a nice normal name, and the same last name as Cookie, she'd decided to reinvent herself completely. And thus Rain Forest was born. Not that the hippie moniker didn't suit her, but Cookie felt ridiculous using it.

"A pleasure," the sheriff said as they shook.

"Same here," Rain replied, clearly on her best

behavior. "Cookie's told me so much about you, about how nice you've been to her, and how warm and friendly you all have been." She was laying it on a bit thick, no doubt going for the sweet, older-lady vibe.

"Glad to hear it," she replied. "Your daughter's been a real asset around here, helped us out a bunch of times already."

Cookie let out some tension she hadn't realized she'd been holding. Last time she'd been in in the office, the sheriff had told her she needed to get fingerprinted. She'd been deputized to help with the Dickie Dungworth case, and it was standard protocol. The only problem was, checking her prints would come back with her real name and the fact that she'd been FBI and had walked out of the job. Hunter had come to her rescue by telling Watkins that Cookie couldn't be fingerprinted, but that he'd cleared her. He'd implied that she'd been his CI back in Philly, not realizing that this would suggest she'd been a lowlife, an addict, or worse. He'd promised Cookie that he'd correct any misapprehensions and make it clear that she'd been a respectable citizen who'd risked her own life to help bring someone to justice. Judging by the warmth of Watkins's tone, he'd made good on his promise.

Which meant that Cookie didn't have to worry about having her cover blown. "That's actually kind of why I'm here," she said. "Do you have a minute to talk in private?"

"Of course." Her face became stern, and it was

impressive how Watkins could go from grandmotherly to tough professional cop in a heartbeat. "Why don't we step into my office?"

"Sounds great. Mom, wait right here, okay?" Cookie said.

Rain pressed her lips together in a thin line, clearly not pleased, but she nodded anyway.

Cookie almost laughed. Maybe it was a little cruel to leave Rain standing around in a sheriff's office, but at least she knew her mother couldn't get up to any trouble there.

Watkins led the way back to her office, which was glass-walled like the rest of the station so that she could see what was going on throughout the entire place from her desk. The Sheriff perched on the edge of that desk to face Cookie. "What's this all about?" she asked, all business.

"Did Deputy Swan call you?" Cookie asked. When the sheriff shook her head, Cookie launched into a short explanation of what had happened so far—the lobster trap, the drugs, the package, the hand. "Dr. Delgado is running tests on the hand now," she concluded, "and Hunter's already on his way out, since drug trafficking makes it a federal case." Of course, it could just as easily fall under DEA jurisdiction, or shared between them now that there was a probable murder as well, but that would be up to Hunter and Watkins to decide. Like most agents, Hunter didn't like having to share with the other agencies if he could avoid it. Cookie knew he'd push to keep it strictly FBI and local law, and she had the feeling Watkins would go along with his decision.

"Oh, Agent O'Neil is coming back? That's very nice." Watkins's hand went to her bun, probably without conscious thought, and Cookie did her best not to smile. The sheriff had a very obvious crush on Hunter, which was sweet and utterly unrequited. It didn't interfere with her job at all, however, as she continued, "Since you're already on the case, why don't I just deputize you again, in order to keep everything nice and legal?"

"That would be great," Cookie replied. Knowing that she had the legal authority to make arrests would definitely put her more at ease. Although as Watkins swore her in and handed her a deputy's badge, Cookie could practically hear Dylan in her head.

Just couldn't stay away, could you?

Cookie fingered the sharp edges of her new badge as she pushed his voice out of her head. It wasn't her fault drugs had washed up on the shore, or that a hand had shown up at her house. Was it?

"Keep me posted," Watkins instructed as they exited her office and retraced their steps to where Rain waited. "And be careful. Sounds like whoever's behind this is serious and not likely to stop at half-measures."

"Got it." Cookie nodded as she steered her mother toward the doors. "Thanks."

"Nice to meet you," Rain called back as they left, lifting a hand in farewell. "Is she still watching us?" she whispered to Cookie once they were outside.

"No, Mom," Cookie replied, not even bothering to glance back. There was no doubt Sheriff Watkins had better things to do than watch them go. "You're fine. Relax."

"Whew! She reminded me of a bulldog, that woman," Rain said, a small shudder running through her. "I half-expected her to sniff me for drugs."

"Why would she do that?" Cookie asked, eyeing her mother. "She wouldn't have found any, right?" When her mother didn't reply, she stopped and glared at Rain. "Right?"

Sheepishly, Rain stuck a hand in her pocket and pulled out a lollipop. An oddly green-shaded lollipop. Cookie couldn't believe it. She'd seen those before. Rain and her friend Winter had cooked them up using pot they'd bought off Stone Harris. "Mom!" she cried, then stopped, glanced around, and lowered her voice. "You brought a pot lolly to a police station?"

"Well, I didn't know that's where we were going," her mother snapped back. "And it was only in case of emergencies."

Cookie sighed and shook her head. "Next time, leave the drugs at home, okay? Or better yet, get rid of them. Geez, you're a menace," she said, already knowing there was no changing Rain. She'd given up on that one long ago.

"I'll just leave them in my underwear drawer," her mother said with a smirk. "I could invite Jared over and have a little treasure hunt. There's nothing like a sexy man putting his hands all over my unmentionables." She smiled, her concerns magically vanishing in the wake of her lust haze. "So, where to next?"

10.

"NEXT?" COOKIE FROWNED at her mother as they strolled past a collection of commercial offices. A light, salt-scented breeze blew off the bay. "What do you mean, next? This isn't the start of the 'Cookie and Rain Adventure Hour'. You asked to go with me to drop off the severed hand, you did, and now it's back to the inn with you."

Two women, who were both dressed in capris and matching sweater sets, paused and turned to stare at Cookie when she uttered the words *severed hand*. Their eyes were wide as their mouths gaped.

Cookie gave them a wan smile and kept walking. Secret Seal Isle might be so small that everybody knew everybody else's business, but Hancock was practically a teeming metropolis by comparison, and she was confident most of the people who saw her now would never see her again. There was no reason to stop an explain.

Besides, she had bigger problems. Namely, her

mother, who was now pouting and stamping her foot in a mock tantrum. "You promised I could come with you," Rain declared. Cookie was shocked that her lower lip didn't tremble as she said it.

"For this one errand," Cookie corrected. "Which you did. And that's done. The end."

"But what about the rest of the case?" Rain asked. "Are you really going to shut me out of it just like that? After the shock I've had? The terror I endured?" She pressed, really laying it on thick. Unbelievable. And her eyes were actually welling up with tears. *How the hell does she do that on command*, Cookie wondered. She'd never been able to tear up for effect. She only cried when it was damned inconvenient, but Rain could turn it on and off like a trained actress. Which probably shouldn't have been that big a surprise, seeing as how her mother had been putting on one performance after another her entire life.

"You're fine, Mom," Cookie pointed out. "You're clearly over it. What is it you're really after here?" She set her hands on her hips. "Spill."

Her mother did her best to hold the hurt look, but finally sighed and dropped it, the shattered expression sliding off her face like water off a duck's back. "I'm bored, okay?" she answered. "We don't have any guests, I don't really know anybody on the island—well, okay, I know a few people, but most of them are busy during the day. And besides, all they want to talk about are lobsters and fishing and each other. I'm going stir-crazy." She beamed up at Cookie, and for once it looked genuine. "This is fun. Mother-daughter bonding and solving crime at the same time. How cool is that?"

Cookie started to reply, then stopped. She'd wanted to go into law enforcement ever since she was a kid, and although Rain had tried to talk her out of it initially, once she saw that Cookie was serious, she'd supported her dreams. She'd always done her best to provide Cookie with whatever she needed to succeed. But she'd never taken an active involvement in her career, mainly because she had such an innate aversion for officers, agents, and anything revolving around the law. This was the first time that Rain had ever been interested in what Cookie did or one of her cases. Sure, Rain didn't know all the details. And sure, it had almost literally been dumped in her lap, so she was already involved, sort of. Even so, it actually was kind of nice to not have Rain turning up her nose and saying, 'Oh, you're working,' and shut out anything more.

So maybe it wouldn't be so bad to let Rain tag along for a little while?

"All right," Cookie said finally. "You really want to help me with this?"

Rain nodded eagerly. She was practically vibrating she was so excited. And Cookie thought it looked like the real deal.

"Fine. But," Cookie warned, "you follow my lead, got it?"

"Got it!" A huge grin stretched across Rain's face,

and she lunged forward to wrap Cookie in a tight hug. "Thank you, sweetie! This is going to be so much fun."

Already, Cookie was starting to second-guess her decision, but she soldiered on. "It isn't all fun and games," she told her as she peeled her mother's surprisingly strong arms off herself. "You know what most cop shows and detective movies never show you? That ninety percent of the work is in the research."

"Research?" Rain made a face, but quickly wiped it away when she saw Cookie's frown. "Right, research. What are we researching? I'm on it." She pulled out her phone and held it up, clearly ready to Google the hell out of something.

Cookie laughed. "Call me old-fashioned, but I'd rather read my results on a screen I can actually see," she answered. She put her hand on her mother's shoulder and steered her farther down the street. "Come on." Fortunately Hancock was still small enough that they could get to her planned destination by foot, since they'd gotten rid of their car when they'd first arrived on Secret Seal Isle. The occasional cab zoomed by, as well, but it was a nice morning, clear and bright, so Cookie figured they might as well get some exercise. And maybe the trek would keep her mom occupied for a bit.

"Can we at least have code names?" Rain asked as they started to walk again. "I'll be Sexy Mama. You can be"—she pursed her lips, thinking—"oh, Back-talking Offspring. Or, no, Mama's Girl. Perfect!" Rain giggled.

Cookie wondered if, now that she'd been deputized

again, she could shoot her mother and get away with it. Nothing serious, just a flesh wound, something to slow her down so Cookie could make a clean getaway.

"Here?" Rain stopped in the middle of the sidewalk, staring up at the large, handsome stone building in front of them. Then she turned and scowled at Cookie, like this was some big joke on her. "Are you serious?"

"Absolutely," Cookie answered. "You wanted to see how this works? Well, welcome to the dazzling world of investigation." She put a hand on her mother's back, right between the shoulder blades, and gave her a gentle but firm push. "Now, in we go."

Rain's thundercloud expression did not abate as she grudgingly let herself be propelled up the steps and into the Hancock Public Library. The scent of dust and old paper, as well as the quiet of the space, was like music to Cookie's senses. As she'd hoped, the library had several computers set aside for public use. In fact, it had an entire room of them, a nice big sunny room with bay windows taking up much of the far wall. The computers were arranged in little clusters, three to a group, so that even if you looked around you wouldn't be able to see more than one or two other screens. There didn't seem to be a sign-up sheet, or a time limit. Instead there was a notice posted on the wall near the entrance. *Please be considerate of other users—keep the volume down, and if others are waiting, do not dawdle.* It was perfect.

Only a handful of other people were using the computers, so Cookie was able to snag one of the machines closest to the windows. She grabbed the chair from the next computer and carried it over so that both she and Rain could sit together, then opened the machine's Internet browser. "All right," she said, "what do we know so far?"

"We know that somebody chopped off a man's hand and mailed it to you," Rain replied, lowering her voice at Cookie's frantic gesture. "Sorry."

"Hmm, but that's not really true, is it?" Cookie pointed out, thinking about what her mother had just said. She twirled a strand of her silky hair around her finger. "The first part is, sure, and Jared—Doctor Delgado—is looking to see what he can tell us about the hand, the man it came from, and even how it was cut off. But it didn't come by regular mail, which is probably for the best because, gross. It came by courier."

Rain brightened. "That's right. Cute Delivery Guy."

"I don't suppose you caught the name of the company?" Cookie asked, and she wasn't surprised when her mother shook her head.

"Nope, sorry. I was more interested in his package than his uniform." Rain smirked.

"Of course you were." Cookie rolled her eyes while stifling a chuckle. It was hard not to be amused by her mother's one-track mind sometimes. "Well, there can't be that many courier companies around here." The keys of the computer clicked as Cookie pulled up a local directory and typed in *courier service*. Five company names appeared, and she pulled out her phone. "Now we start calling."

"Calling? Pshaw! Let me at this thing." Rain dragged the keyboard closer to her and began typing in search commands. "Let's see," she muttered as pecked away at the keyboard. "Cute, dark hair, nice tush, delivery, mysterious package, and—Voila!"

Even as warning bells went off in Cookie's head her mother hit Enter and ran the search.

Instantly, the computer screen began to fill with window after window after window of x-rated content. New ones popped up so fast their contents barely registered before they were blotted out by the next. But what little Cookie did see of them was likely be burned into her brain forever. Especially since some of those windows had sound. She hurriedly switched off the computer's speakers, but not before a series of moans and groans and cries filled the room.

Heads swiveled in their direction, and a young assistant librarian stationed off to one side rose to his feet and quickly headed toward them. He stopped, though, when he saw that it was two women sitting at the computer and looked even more confused when Cookie mouthed "sorry" at him. It was clear that he'd had far less apologetic encounters over similar material. And after a second, he simply nodded and returned to his post, evidently trusting Cookie and her mother to protect their own virtue.

Rain was oblivious, of course. "Oh!" she said, avidly watching the screen. "Well, that's a good package, all right. And he is dressed as a delivery boy, but I don't think they really do that, do they? If so, we've been ordering from the wrong places." She tilted her head as she studied the screen. "Hmm, now that's nice, I haven't really seen something like that in a while. Maybe—"

"Mom!" Cookie grabbed the mouse and tried her best to kill each window, but they were popping up too fast for her to keep up. Finally, she gave up and killed the browser instead. It still spawned at least three more ads before it died, and she leaned back in her chair with a sigh. "What were you thinking?" she demanded after a second, careful to keep her voice down to a hushed whisper. "We're looking up couriers, not delivery-guy porn."

"I didn't even realize there was a delivery-guy category," Rain insisted, though she didn't look the least bit embarrassed about finding it. Then she arched an eyebrow. "But it appears you did. The question is how? Care to explain, dear?" she asked with a knowing smirk.

"Lucky freaking guess," Cookie growled back. She rebooted the browser, ran the search again, and readied her phone. "Now let's do this the right way," she declared, dialing the first number. "Hello, is this ABC Deliveries?" she asked after the call had connected. "Hi, I'm Cookie James. I'm with the Hancock Sheriff's Office, and I was wondering if I could ask you a few questions?"

"Boring," Rain muttered beside her, crossing her arms. "At least let me go back to those other sites while you do this. Some of those videos seemed quite...informative."

Cookie ignored her, but did scoop both the mouse and keyboard off the desk and into her lap for safekeeping.

11.

UNFORTUNATELY, EVEN WITHOUT interference from Rain, the phone calls wound up being unproductive.

"I thought they had to answer your questions," Rain huffed as the two of them gathered their things and exited the library. Cookie pointedly ignored the assistant librarian's judgmental parting glare, and the way he eyed them the whole way out the door as if he was afraid they were going to steal something. But she didn't miss the way the way he scrambled behind them and shut the door with a solid thud. "Isn't that the whole point of being the law?" her mother continued. "That people have to do what you say and tell you the truth and all that?"

Cookie cast a sidelong glance at her mother. "When has that ever worked on you?" she asked, raising an eyebrow. "Most of the time, it makes you do the exact opposite."

Rain didn't even try to deny that. "Well, sure," she replied instead. "But that's me. We're talking regular people here." That made Cookie laugh, especially since it was true. Nobody who'd ever met Rain would call her regular.

"Most people do want to stay on our good side," Cookie agreed. "But how far they'll go to get there is different from person to person. Some will tell me anything and everything, right down to their cup size, what they had for breakfast, and how many donuts they snuck from the corporate break room. Others will answer the basics, and they'll stay polite, but without a court order?" She shrugged. "It's all 'protecting the clients' privacy' and 'looking out for our employees' and so on."

Which was exactly what she'd gotten from all five of the places she'd called. All of them had been perfectly pleasant on the phone. All of them had been apologetic. And all of them had basically said, "get a court order and we'll show you our records, otherwise forget about it."

And naturally, she couldn't get a court order. Not for something like this. If she suspected that one of these companies had an employee who had committed a serious crime, like if she thought the delivery guy had been the one to kill whomever that hand belonged to, then she could get a court order. But only if she could show enough evidence to either prove they were involved or at least make it reasonably likely. Since, as far as she knew, the killer had simply hired the courier to deliver the package, she had no leverage on the company. She hadn't even been able to get any of the companies to confirm that they'd been the one to deliver it, which would have at least given her a place to start. But even though she'd been the recipient, they insisted that they'd need to be ordered to divulge their records.

Which meant, at least for now, the courier angle was a waste of time. So Cookie thought, but Rain, it turned out, had other ideas.

"I know!" she announced, stopping on the sidewalk and snapping her fingers. "We could go to Winter's."

"Winter's tea shop?" Winter was one of Rain's oldest friends, from back in her real hippie days, and it turned out she had a 'medicinal' tea shop here in Hancock. Which Cookie hadn't known until Winter had shown up at the inn one evening to hang out with Rain. Rain claimed it was a total coincidence and that she'd only discovered it that same day. But Cookie suspected that was a lie, and that Winter's presence here had strongly influenced Rain's suggestion that they head up to Maine in general and this area in particular.

Not that Cookie disliked Winter. She'd known the older woman since childhood, but Winter was just as flakey as Rain. And together, well, the two of them were trouble.

Right now, though, Cookie was puzzled. "Why would Winter know anything about any of this?" she asked. Of course, Winter liked to get high as much as Rain did, but even if Rain had known about the drug aspect of this case, which Cookie was still reasonably sure she did not, these illegal drugs were a very different beast, and she couldn't see Winter going anywhere near that stuff.

But Rain's answer had nothing to do with drugs. "Winter knows everybody," she explained. "If anybody can tell us who my hot delivery guy is, it's her."

Cookie considered that. It actually wasn't a bad plan. She'd certainly used Rain's similar knowledge of Secret Seal Isle and its inhabitants to locate persons of interest in the other two cases she'd worked over the past month. And since they were already in town and she didn't have any other leads, what did they have to lose? "Okay, sure," she said. "Let's go see Winter."

From her mother's squeal, you'd have thought Cookie had just promised to take her on a shopping spree or to a high-end spa or something. Or maybe that Rain and Winter hadn't seen each other in years, when in fact they'd gotten together just a few days ago. But at least it made her mother happy.

Winter's shop wasn't hard to find. It was close to the docks, as was everything else in this coastal town, and the second Cookie saw it she knew it had to be the right place. The large, wooden, teapot-shaped sign hung from an iron post just above the front door. *The Tea Tripper* was written in flouncy script that made her think of Alice in Wonderland.

Rain led the way up the front steps, then pushed open the wide, curve-topped front door with its cheerful stained-glass panels. A set of wind chimes tinkled merrily at their entrance.

"Hello?" Rain called out. She paused just inside the

door, and then tried again, sounding a little surprised. "Hello? Winter?"

Cookie was right behind her, and suddenly the hair on the back of her neck stood up. She put one hand under the back of her shirt to grasp the butt of her pistol. It did seem awfully quiet in here. Especially for Winter.

But then there was a loud bustling from the back of the store, and a second later a large, heavyset older woman came barreling into the room, her long silvery braid flying behind her. "Rain! Cookie!" Winter called out as she rushed forward to scoop each of them up into a massive bear hug that made Cookie's back crack. "How are you both?" She released the women, and Cookie's unease vanished.

"Welcome to The Tea Tripper!" Winter spread her arms and spun around, clearly very proud of her commercial enterprise.

Now that Cookie had a second to look around, she could see this place was one hundred percent Winter. The shop looked like—well, it looked like someone had taken a nice, quiet, cozy little tea shop and then gone on a wild bender before deciding to redecorate in a drugged-out sixties motif. Lava lamps stood in many of the corners. Gods-eyes and dream-catchers decorated most of the windows. Beaded curtains hung across several of the aisles, while batiks covered the walls and the ceiling. Then there were brightly colored throw pillows tucked away in wicker cubbies, and long strands of beads, colored lights, and leis dangled along the tops of the windows.

Cookie also couldn't help noticing that the row of specialty teas arranged behind the counter all had fanciful names like Dreamweaver and State of Zen and Astral Delight. She was willing to bet they did not list their ingredients, because at least a few of those likely included substances that would not pass an FDA inspection.

The glass-fronted counter also held a variety of teacups, teapots, tea balls, and other tea paraphernalia. Behind them were hookahs and what looked suspiciously like hash pipes tucked in back. Still, Cookie nodded. "It's very nice," she assured the older woman. "And it's got your personality all over it."

Winter beamed at Cookie's praise.

"What can I get you two?" Winter asked them, guiding them through a curtained doorway and into a second room, which had been outfitted like a little café with tables and chairs arranged in small groups. "Some tea? Scones? Biscuits? Maybe a few finger sandwiches?"

A small chalkboard on the wall listed the tea shop's food and drink offerings, and Cookie frowned at one of the items. "Blissful Brownies?" she said aloud. "Are those—?"

Rain started to deny it, but Winter had even less tact than she did. "Oh, yes," she agreed right away. "The brownies your mother and I came up with that night back at the inn. They're a huge hit, too. Would you like one?" If she was being facetious at all, Cookie honestly couldn't tell.

"No, thanks," she answered. "I'm sort of on duty. And we actually came to see if you could help us with something."

"Ooh." Her face lit up with excitement. "Do tell!" Winter ushered them to a table by the window and disappeared to get them tea. Cookie glanced at the few other customers seated nearby who were drinking hot beverages and eating cookies or brownies. All of them appeared suitably zoned out.

Winter returned with a pot of tea, a plate of cookies, and three cups that rattled as she set them down at the table.

"Thanks." Cookie hadn't realized that she was starting to get a little peckish, and the pastries did look good. So after first sniffing the drink to make sure it was legal, she poured herself a cup of tea and snagged a butter cookie. "We're trying to find somebody, and we were hoping you might know who he is."

"He's a real cutie," Rain put in, taking what looked like a white-chocolate chunk cookie for herself. "Works as a courier. Tall, slim, dark curly hair, nice nose, brown eyes, chipped front tooth, nice butt. Ring any bells?"

"No, but I'd sure like him too," Winter declared, and she and Rain both giggled like schoolgirls. Which was what always happened whenever they were together. They suddenly turned into pre-teens again.

"We're serious, Winter," Cookie told her after devouring her treat. The buttery goodness was too much to resist, and she reached for another. "It would be a big help if you could identify him."

"Gotcha." Winter sat back and thought, her brow creased, but after a minute she shook her head. "I really don't know anyone who fits that description. Sorry."

"Do you know anybody at any of the courier agencies here in town?" Cookie asked.

"A few," Winter answered. "Mostly at Ace Deliveries, a couple at Speedy Couriers. Nobody who sounds like that, though." She gave Rain a conspiratorial look. "Sounds like you lucked out."

"Only if I can find him again," Rain replied, winking back. "We barely had time to exchange hellos."

"Talking is overrated anyway, right, Rain?" her friend teased, making both of them snicker again, and Cookie rolled her eyes. Why was it that they were twice her age, but she was the one who wound up feeling like a disapproving matron whenever she was around them both? "What was the name of that one you told me about from the other week?" Winter asked Rain and then threw a knowing glance at Cookie. "You know, the one from the shed?"

"Oh, you mean Anthony? He's nice enough. Rain waggled her eyebrows. "And certainly *eager*." Rain glanced to Cookie. "You remember him, don't you?"

"A whole lot more than I ever wanted to," Cookie replied, making the two older women howl with laughter even as she shuddered. It had been during Hunter's first visit here, and the first case she'd wound up falling into on the island. She and Hunter had been talking and had heard strange noises coming from the side of the house. They'd gone to investigate, guns drawn, only to find Rain in the shed, 'entertaining' a male friend. Cookie had been horrified; Hunter had been traumatized; and the man, Anthony, had been embarrassed. But Rain? She'd thought it was funny. And had evidently told Winter all about it.

"Are you still seeing him at all?" Winter was asking.

"Not anything regular, no," Cookie's mother answered. "I think he'd like it to be more frequent, but while he's fine for a bit of fun, I'm not sure about anything more. He's a little unstable, and I think he makes bad life choices." Cookie thought that was pretty funny, coming from her mother, but she chose not to pursue it. It just wasn't worth the headache.

"Sorry I can't help more," Winter told her, patting her hand. "I'll keep my eyes and ears open, and if I see anybody who fits that description, I'll give you a holler." Then she leered a bit. "Though I might try him out myself, first."

Some women would have gotten possessive, claiming they'd spotted him first, but Rain just chuckled. "Go right ahead," she said cheerfully. "You know I like it when they've been broken in." While the older women laughed, Cookie tried to focus entirely on her tea and a third cookie. When she got home, she was going to have to scrub her brain by binge-watching something mindless on Netflix.

Fortunately, the front-door chime sounded. "Oops,

more customers, gotta go," Winter said, heaving herself out of her chair. "Feel free to stick around if you'd like. Have some more cookies, finish off the pot. My treat." Then she disappeared through the curtain toward the front room.

Cookie and Rain did drink a little more tea, but skipped the pastries. After a few minutes they got up and retraced their steps to leave. Winter was behind the counter talking to a customer, but waved at them as they headed out.

"Guess that was a bust, huh?" Rain asked when they were back outside.

"Not entirely," Cookie answered. "It sounds like our guy isn't from Ace or Speedy, so that narrows the list down, which is something, anyway. Maybe when Hunter gets here, he and I can visit the other three. Often people will admit things in person that they won't over the phone. We'll see." She shrugged. "It was a nice break, anyway."

Rain nodded. "And we found out the brownies are doing well." She smiled. "If they keep on selling, we won't have to worry so much about the inn."

Cookie managed to smile back. She was pleased that her mother had found another way to pay the bills, since neither of them had a job outside the inn itself and business hadn't exactly been booming there. She just wished Rain's method didn't involve baked goods with questionable ingredients.

Still, it could have been worse. Cookie remembered a

few of the jobs her mother had held down while she was growing up and shuddered again. At least living on the island meant she didn't have to worry about Rain collecting tips at the local strip club… for now anyway.

12.

COOKIE SMILED AND stepped forward, pushing off the railing she'd been leaning against. She made her way toward the sleek black Mustang that had just pulled off the evening ferry, tossing her hair back as she walked. The nighttime breeze blew her locks out behind her in what was probably more of a frenzied mass than a sexy wave, but she was going with it. As she neared the car, which had slowed at her approach, the driver-side window hummed as it slowly descended. A dark, shadowy figure was visible within the vehicle.

"Hey there, stranger. Looking for a private tour?" Cookie tugged up the collar of her shirt in what she hoped was a cross between a seductive tease and a private detective pose and leaned forward, resting her arms on the window.

"Hey, Charlie." Hunter O'Neil smiled at her from behind the wheel. "Want a lift back?" He looked tired, and she hoped that wasn't entirely because of her call.

"Sure." She trotted around the car and hopped in the

passenger side. "Hey, Hunter." She couldn't help her grin. "Just can't stay away, huh?"

"How could I?" he answered as he put the car back in gear and turned to follow the road through town and up to the inn. "You've got some kind of crazy crime wave going on around here. I mean, seriously? Murders, kidnappings, blackmail, and now heavy-duty drug busts? What, you couldn't come back to Philly so you decided to bring all the crime out here?" She could tell from his tone and the set of his eyes and his jaw that he was only half-kidding.

"I didn't exactly advertise 'hey, former FBI agent here, bring all your crime to me," she reminded him. She slapped him on the arm, but not hard enough to disturb his grip on the wheel. "You know that, right?"

Hunter sighed. "I do, yeah, of course. But you've got to admit, this is some crazy stuff over here." He shook his head. "So fill me in. What's the latest?"

"Let's see." She tapped her fingers on the leather seat. "What do you know already? The drugs, right? The hand." Cookie filled in the details of her grisly package, the note, and what Jared had been able to discern so far. "Should know more once he's had a chance to run some tests," she finished. "I've tried finding out who our courier was, but Mom didn't get his name or his company, and so far I've hit a dead end with all the local companies. They won't divulge without a warrant."

Hunter nodded. "We could try to get one, I suppose," he mused aloud, "but no guarantee we would.

Whoever the courier is, he's probably not involved, so we don't really have sufficient cause to go poking around their confidential files."

"I know." Hunter accelerated a little as they turned up the hill, and then they were pulling up in front of the inn. Cookie smiled as he cut the engine. "You know, you're rapidly becoming our most regular guest. Too bad you're not a paying one."

He quirked an eyebrow at her. "Maybe you should advertise the whole death-and-danger thing," he suggested with a smirk. "That'd probably draw the tourists in by droves."

"Only if you promise to be the token man in uniform," she teased.

"Um, not likely," he said dryly.

She snorted in amusement. They both climbed out of the car and Cookie paused, putting a hand on his arm as he came around. "Oh, one other thing." She stole a quick glance up at the inn and its lit but currently empty front door. "My mom knows about the hand, obviously, and the note, but not about the drugs."

That earned her another raised eyebrow. "How'd you manage that?"

She shrugged. "Snuck them into the shed and buried them in the freezer, under the hand," she answered, keeping her voice down. "She won't go near the thing, so I figured they were safe, at least temporarily." Cookie knew with her mother, she'd better keep a close eye on her anyway.

Hunter considered that a second before nodding. "Probably a good call." He knew enough about Rain to understand why Cookie would want to keep the presence of the drugs from her mother, but he was kind enough not to say anything further.

"Why, Agent O'Neil!" Rain magically appeared in the doorway as they were climbing the steps up to the porch. "How nice to see you again." She gave him a big, enthusiastic hug, which Hunter accepted easily enough. "I'm assuming you're here because of Cookie's secret admirer?"

Hunter sent a questioning glance at Cookie, who shrugged.

"You know, because he's sending her these grisly packages with cryptic notes and no name?" Rain laughed. "Come on, I thought you guys were the detectives around here." She turned and headed back inside, calling over her shoulder, "Dinner should be ready in about twenty. Cookie, I've arranged his usual room for him."

"Thanks, Mom." Cookie did her best not to grit her teeth at how obvious her mother could be. The inn had three floors, and the second floor was currently completely empty. Yet Rain continually insisted on putting Hunter in the only other room on the third floor, which was directly opposite Cookie's own room. Not exactly subtle.

With an apologetic shrug, she led him inside and up the stairs, snagging the key to his room on the way. "It's like you never left," she said as she pushed the door open and stepped aside so he could enter and toss his bag on the bed.

"I might have to just start leaving some clothes here," he joked, looking around the room. It was a great space; high ceiling, hardwood floor, big windows, ceiling fan, and nice old furniture. Very comfortable, with a sort of shabby elegance about it.

Cookie's phone rang, the shrill sound slightly muffled by her jeans pocket. She dug it out and checked the screen, then answered. "Hey, Jared," she said, walking into the room and turning slightly so Hunter could sidle over and listen in. "What's going on?"

Hi, Cookie," the medical examiner answered. "Sorry to call so late. Hope I'm not interrupting dinner or anything, but I figured you'd want the results as soon as I had them."

"Absolutely," she agreed. "What've you got?"

"So the fingerprinting was a total bust," he said. "Sorry. Whoever cut off this hand used acid to burn away any trace of prints."

"Ouch." She winced. That was unfortunate, but there were probably other ways to get an ID on the victim, even if prints would've been the easiest.

"I did find something else interesting, though," he continued. "I ran blood tests, and discovered unusual levels of radioactive isotopes. There were also some trace chemicals, pretty nasty ones. So either your victim worked at both a nuclear power plant and a chemical factory, or he had cancer."

"Cancer?" She glanced up to meet Hunter's eyes over the phone. "Ah, because he'd had both radiation therapy and chemo?"

"Exactly. I can't tell what kind, not skin, or at least if it was it wasn't in the hand. But whatever it was, judging from these levels, I'm guessing it was pretty advanced."

"Got it. Thanks." That was certainly something to go on. She was already picturing calling the hospital in Hancock and asking about any cancer patients that might fit the bill. "Anything else?"

"Yeah, one other thing. He's local."

"How do you know?"

Jared laughed. "I could explain it, but it's pretty technical. Suffice it to say, this guy's skin had traces of seawater, sand, rust, and a few other things that pinpoint his origin to a twenty-mile radius, from Secret Seal to Hancock and just a little past us. It's like the geographic equivalent of a fingerprint."

"Okay. Thanks, Jared. That's a huge help. Goodnight." Cookie hung up and Hunter took a quick step back, putting a more comfortable distance between them. "So we know he's from here, and that he was seriously ill with cancer."

Hunter nodded, thoughtfully. "Anybody you know fit that bill?"

Cookie shook her head. "I can't think of anyone." She grinned. "But I bet I know somebody who can."

Together they traipsed back downstairs. Dishes thudded on the dinning room table as Rain set plates out. "Oh, good timing," she said when she saw them. "I was just about to call you down."

"Whatever you made, it smells amazing, Rain," Hunter told her as he stepped up to the table. And it did. Some kind of pasta dish, Cookie guessed, and seared fish to go with it.

Rain blushed at the compliment. "Thank you, Hunter. That's very sweet of you." She moved toward her favorite chair and started to pull it out, but stopped midway, eyeing them both. "All right, what's going on? Spill it."

"We were just wondering," Cookie asked, keeping her tone as light as she could while reaching for her own seat. Not for the first time she wished her mother wasn't quite so good at reading her. "Do you know anybody here or in Hancock, like maybe one of the lobstermen, who's been really sick lately? Like sick enough to be a regular at the doctor's office?"

Rain's face fell, her good humor instantly turning to sadness. "Oh, you mean Jimmy Calder," she replied. "Poor thing. Lung cancer, stage four, inoperable. He's gone through chemo twice with no result. It's just awful." Cookie knew that this was no act. Her mother might be flaky, and flighty, and sometimes self-centered, but she had a big heart, and she really cared, even about people she'd never met.

"Jimmy Calder." Cookie rolled that name around in her mouth for a second. "He's a lobsterman, right?"

Her mother nodded. "His wife Leslie's a waitress

over at the Tipsy Seagull. Nice people. And he's only in his late forties, much too young for something like this. It's really sad."

Now Cookie remembered where she'd seen his name before. "There's a jar at the Salty Dog," she told Hunter. "Collecting donations to help with his medical bills."

"Most of the local businesses have them," Rain agreed. "He doesn't have any insurance, and it's not like either of them make much money, and chemo's expensive."

Cookie shared a look with Hunter, who nodded. "I hate to have to do this, Rain," he said, taking a step away from the table instead of toward it, "but it sounds like Charlie and I need to go pay a visit to Jimmy's wife. And we'd better do it right away. With this kind of case, the longer you wait, the more evidence can get lost." He favored her with his most charming smile. "I don't suppose you could keep dinner warm for us?"

Like so many women before her, many of whom Cookie had only heard about in morning-after stories, Rain melted under that smile. "Of course I can," she promised. "Just don't be too long, you hear? Otherwise the fish'll get dry."

"We'll be quick as we can, Mom," Cookie told her. "Thanks." She followed Hunter back outside.

She hoped Leslie was working tonight, and that she might have some way for them to confirm that the hand had come from Jimmy.

13.

"HOW'RE YOU HOLDING up with all this?" Hunter asked as they headed down the hill toward the Tipsy Seagull. A cool breeze that bordered on cold blew around them as the evening approached. There was no point in taking the car, since it was only a ten-minute walk and the weather was nice. The only real reason he needed a vehicle at all was for the drive from the nearest airport to Hancock and then onto the ferry.

At first Cookie thought he meant the events of the evening. "Fine," she answered, but even without looking right at him she could tell he was frowning at that. "What? I'm fine."

"Charlie," he said, using the name he'd always had for her. "Somebody sent you a hand in the mail."

"It wasn't regular mail, it was couriered," she replied automatically.

He sighed and she echoed him.

"Okay, okay." She didn't slow down or stop, but she did mentally pause to consider the question seriously.

"I'm okay," she answered finally. "Really. Yeah, it's a little creepy, but we've seen worse."

"Sure, but worse wasn't mailed—sorry, delivered—to your door," Hunter pointed out. "Whoever's doing this is willing to not only kill a man but chop him up and use him for a message. That's hardcore."

"It is, and I really want to get whoever's behind this," she agreed, twisting a little so she could face him better even as they continued to walk. "And yes, I've got my guard up, okay? But otherwise I'm fine."

He didn't reply to that, just studied her for a minute before nodding once. Cookie tried not to show just how relieved she was. She knew full well that Hunter could get protective. It had taken her almost a year to break him of the habit of stepping in front of her to shield her whenever they broke down a door or somebody pulled a gun. That was sweet and all, but it wasn't how equal partners worked. If he treated her like someone who needed protecting, not only was he not able to do his job fully, but he wasn't letting her do hers either. Eventually he'd gotten that message. She hadn't needed a defender then, and she certainly didn't now.

They continued on in silence for a few minutes before Hunter spoke again. "So, this Jimmy Calder," he started. "We're liking him for this?"

Cookie shrugged. "I guess. I don't really know the guy. I've seen him around once or twice, I think, at least the pictures on the jar are sort of familiar, but that's about it. Still, if he had terminal lung cancer and nasty medical bills and wasn't exactly raking in the big bucks as a lobsterman—"

"—he could've turned to drug smuggling to make ends meet, yeah," Hunter agreed. "And then, what, a run went wrong and they killed him?"

"That lobster trap washed up on Lookout Point," Cookie replied. "I'm betting that wasn't deliberate. Apparently it happens sometimes. The chain can break, or a really strong wave can just pick the whole thing up and when you come back out to pull up the trap, it's gone. Which means you've lost whatever it'd caught, but also the trap itself, and they're not cheap to replace."

Hunter nodded. "It's a smart way to smuggle drugs," he said, slowing as they neared the Tipsy Seagull. "A drop-off point out on the water, and nobody knows the exact location but you and your supplier. They load in the drugs and you collect them, deal them, and return their cut of the money."

Cookie laughed and shook her head. "There's no way this guy was a heavy-duty drug dealer," she argued. "Not unless he's only selling to other lobstermen, bar staff, and a couple of local businessmen. He had to have just been the mule, that's all. I bet he never even touched the drugs himself; he just provided the traps so the suppliers could get them safely to the real dealers. And for that he got a cut of the money, probably not much, but a lot more than he'd have made off a trap full of actual lobsters."

Hunter nodded, and smiled. "Always keeping me grounded in reality," he told her. "Just like you used to."

They stopped in front of the Tipsy Seagull, and Hunter puffed up his chest as he got into agent mode. "Ready?"

"Let's do this." Together they stepped up onto the bar's front porch with the solid thud of serious footsteps. While most waterfront establishments would want their decks to face out toward the water, the Tipsy Seagull appeared to have deliberately shunned the stunning views of the bay. Its porch was in front toward the town instead, as if shielding its patrons from the sight of the ocean they worked every day.

When they entered, Cookie was again struck by the difference between the bar's ramshackle exterior and its worn but much more homey interior. Not that it was luxury accommodations or anything, but the inside was clean, far more solid, and far less shabby than the outside would suggest.

There were more people here than usual, though the place was still only half-full. She spotted the bartender, Ian Tremaine, whom they'd interviewed about Chip Winslow's death. He still looked too delicate to be tending bar at a rough-and-tumble place like the Seagull, but it was obvious watching him that he was comfortable here, and the patrons all knew him. There were two waitresses delivering drinks, one of them a slender blonde and the other a stocky redhead. "I bet that one's Leslie Calder," Cookie said softly, nodding toward the blonde.

"Right." Hunter waited for his moment, timing it perfectly. Just as Leslie returned to the bar with an empty serving tray, he stepped forward to intercept her. "Leslie

Calder?" he asked, holding up his badge and ID when she nodded. "I'm Special Agent O'Neil, FBI. I'd like to ask you a few questions, if you have a minute?" He'd always been good at the cool-but-not-mean professional demeanor, and his tone made it clear this wasn't really a request.

Leslie glanced over at Ian, who looked annoyed but nodded, before setting the tray on the bar and following Hunter back toward the door and then outside. It was pleasant out, but all the patrons had decided to hole-up in inside, making the deserted patio the perfect spot for a private conversation. Leslie glanced at Cookie as they stepped out, spotted the deputy's badge Cookie was once again wearing at her belt, and nodded without asking anything.

Leslie was the kind of woman who'd be described as care-worn, Cookie decided as she studied the waitress. What she'd initially taken as slender was actually outright thin; the kind of thin you get from stress and constant work and probably not enough food. The kind that wore away all the fat until you had a vaguely hollowed-out look. Her blond hair was stringy and dull and pulled back into a serviceable bun, and she was unconsciously wringing her serving apron with her hands.

"What's this all about?" Leslie asked with the tone of someone who was used to having life deliver a series of bad breaks. Given her husband's condition, that made total sense.

"We wanted to ask you about your husband,

Jimmy," Hunter started, but Cookie tapped him on the arm before he could get any farther.

"We were hoping to buy some lobsters from him," she finished, deciding at the last minute there wasn't any reason to alarm Leslie until they could ID their still-missing body for certain. Cookie cast Hunter a let-me-handle-this glance and smiled apologetically at Leslie. "Sorry for the badges and all—force of habit. There's no need to be concerned," she lied, wishing with all her heart that it was true.

Leslie was eyeing her like she didn't know what to make of all this. "You want to buy lobsters from Jimmy?" she asked slowly. "An FBI agent and a deputy? For what, exactly?"

"Oh, we've got a cookout," Cookie replied easily, trying to act like this was the most normal thing in the world. "Agent O'Neil here is in town for a few days, following up on the Winslow case." Everyone in town knew about that, so it wasn't a surprise when the waitress nodded at the reference. "And Sheriff Watkins thought it'd be nice to treat him to some local hospitality." She lowered her voice, letting the actual sympathy she felt for Leslie rise to the fore. "We thought, well, if we had to get lobsters somewhere, we might as well get them from your husband, you know? Put a little more money in your pockets?"

That did the trick. Tears came to Leslie's eyes, and the smile she offered in return was sad and grateful. "That's very kind of you," she said, looking from Cookie to Hunter and back again. "Thank you. Jimmy's out on his boat right now, but I can tell him as soon as he returns."

"He's out on his boat?" Hunter asked. He frowned up at the night sky. "Isn't it kind of late for that sort of thing? I honestly have no idea. I'm not much of a boat person." He spread his hands wide as if to apologize for his ignorance.

"It is late," she admitted, "but Jimmy's been pulling a lot of long hours lately." She glanced down at her hands, which she'd clasped together. "Truth is...well, truth is, we're going to Paris."

"What?" Cookie leaned in, not sure at first if she'd heard correctly. "You're going to Paris? As in, Paris, France?" The idea of this woman walking the streets of Paris, which admittedly, Cookie had never seen herself, just didn't compute.

But now Leslie's smile was genuine, and maybe just a little bit proud. "That's right," she replied, raising her chin. "Me and Jimmy. We'd always talked about it, you know, like you do, but once he got sick..." Her voice dropped again, as did her eyes. "Once he got sick, we figured that was never gonna happen. Then, after the last round of chemo, when they said he was done for, he looked me right in the eye and he said, 'Leslie,' he said, 'we're gonna make that trip to Paris if it's the last thing I do. I wanna give you at least one good memory of me to hold onto.'" Her voice wavered, thick with tears. "As if I didn't have a million good memories already," she sobbed as she scrubbed at her eyes with the back of one hand.

"I'm so sorry." Cookie offered her a tissue, which Leslie gratefully accepted. "That sounds amazing. So that's why he's working extra, to pay for the trip?"

Leslie nodded, still dabbing at her eyes. "I'm pulling doubles and triples here, all the shifts they'll give me, and he's working twice as much out on the water, getting every last lobster he can." This time her smile was a little tremulous, as if uncertain whether it should broaden or collapse. "It means we don't get to see each other much for the moment, but we're so close now. Jimmy says once he's finished this latest run we can probably buy our tickets as early as next week."

Cookie's heart went out to this poor woman who'd already been fending off her grief by clinging to this once-in-a-lifetime experience, and who had no idea yet that it would never happen, or that she would never see her husband again. "That's got to be hard," Cookie said, grateful she was able to keep her voice mostly steady. Hopefully the waitress would attribute the slight wobbliness to general sympathy. "When was the last time you actually saw each other?"

Leslie had to stop and think about that one for a second or two. "Sunday morning," she answered finally. "I was just getting in from working all night, and he was just heading out." She smiled, the corners of her eyes glistening again. "But we'll be together the whole time in Paris."

"Of course." Cookie nodded automatically, forcing herself to keep her smile in place. "Well, if you could just tell him when you see him, that'd be great. Thanks."

The waitress smiled at her, and reached out to grab Cookie's hand with one of hers and Hunter's with the other. "Thank you. It's meant so much to us, having all this support from everyone." She let them go again after a second, and waved as she turned to go back in to work. "I'll definitely let him know, and we'll set aside the best ones out of the catch for you."

"That would be great," Hunter assured her. "Thank you again."

They watched her leave. Once the door shut behind her, they both let out heavy sighs. "Sometimes," Hunter muttered, "I really hate this job."

"Yeah," was all Cookie could say in reply, because that pretty much covered it all.

14.

"ALL RIGHT, WHAT now?" Cookie asked after Leslie had gone. "We're pretty sure who our victim is, even if we can't prove it yet. And we have a working theory of what happened to him and why. But we still don't know who did it, or where the body is or anything else we need to close this case." Now that she'd seen the completely unsuspecting widow, she wanted to find and punish the people responsible for Jimmy's death more than ever.

Hunter ran a hand over his smooth scalp, something he only did when he was thinking, and usually only when he was considering things that went outside the normal FBI playbook. "That depends," he replied slowly. "How adventurous are you feeling?"

Cookie knew exactly what that meant. Hunter was planning something potentially stupid and possibly illegal. She grinned up at him. "What've you got in mind?"

He smiled back and pulled out his phone. "Once

your mom told us about Jimmy, I ran a background check on him." He held up the phone to show her the screen. "I've got his home address."

"And his wife is working late again tonight," Cookie completed the thought. "Which means his house should be empty right now."

"Nothing we find will be admissible," Hunter reminded her, though of course he was aware she knew that. He was just making sure they both understood exactly what they were doing here. They were talking about an unlawful entry and an illegal search. It was the kind of thing that could easily get you tossed from the Bureau.

Fortunately, she didn't work for the FBI anymore. And she was the only person who'd ever know what Hunter had done. "If we find something to point us in the right direction, it'll be worth it," she answered, and he nodded. They were on the same page, as had usually been the case. It was why they made such good partners. They thought enough alike that they could usually follow each other's logic. At the same time, they usually managed to come up with different angles on the same situation, which often led to useful connections and clues.

Cookie checked the address again. Fortunately, Secret Seal Isle wasn't that big. There was the one main street and a few small offshoots and that was it, at least in the residential and commercial part of town. The artist colony on the other end of the island was its own separate community, and she was less familiar with that area. But figuring out where Jimmy and Leslie's house was? That was easy.

When they reached the address, Cookie wasn't surprised to find a weathered but neatly maintained little house. It looked exactly as she'd pictured it would, a tidy little home for a childless couple who both worked full-time but still cared about having a clean, comfortable space for themselves. There were flowers in the front yard, and the walk was swept. The paint on the shutters had started to peel but not so badly that they needed repainting yet. A cheery *The Calders* sign hung on the front door, and a *Welcome to our happy home* door mat right in front of that.

"Shall we?" Hunter asked as they approached the porch. She nodded, and he reached out and rapped on the door with one hand. "Hello?" he called out. "Anybody home? This is FBI Special Agent Hunter O'Neil, and I'd like to ask you some questions." Nobody answered. After trying again, he reached for the doorknob. It didn't turn. Locked.

"What, you thought they'd make it that easy?" Cookie asked with a smirk. She elbowed him out of the way and pulled a pair of bobby pins from her pocket. She kept them handy in case she needed to pin her hair out of her eyes, but also because they made excellent lock picks. And she'd always been better at breaking and entering than Hunter, thanks to a certain larcenous ex-boyfriend from her high school days. It was good to know Tommy Malloy had ultimately been good for something.

The lock gave way within seconds, allowing her to push the door open and usher Hunter inside. He grunted but stepped in, moving aside so she could follow and close the door again behind her. No sense advertising their presence to the neighbors.

Cookie was still letting her eyes adjust when she heard a quick pitter-patter approaching them, and then a low growl. Oh crap. Just what they needed, a guard dog.

She turned and glanced toward the hall just as a large, broad-shouldered brown-and-white shape came barreling through the doorway. He had floppy ears, heavy jowls, a squared face, and big dark eyes that were fixed on them. His tail was straight up, and his jowls pulled back to show a mouth full of impressive teeth.

"Whoa," Hunter muttered. Then he added, a bit louder, "Nice doggie."

The dog growled louder in response.

Again, Cookie hip-checked her ex-partner to the side. "I've got this," she told him. "Animals love me."

"Love you like they want to be your friend, or love you like you're their favorite appetizer?" Hunter asked, though he stepped back, giving her the lead.

"Hopefully the first one," she admitted quietly as she squatted down and held out her hand. "Hey there, handsome," she told the dog, who was now only a few feet away. "How're you? My name's Cookie. What's yours?"

The dog's eyes remained fixed on her, but she saw his ears twitch as her words reached him. A second later, he crept forward, his nose only inches from her hand. He was still showing his teeth, but he'd stopped growling, which she took for a good sign. His tail twitched a little, and her lips curved into a gentle smile.

"That's a good boy," she told him softly, her hand still out. The dog sniffed her fingers, then finally nudged his nose into her hand, his tail wagging.

She blew out a breath, relief running through her. She shifted her hand to run it up his forehead, scratching him behind the ears as he closed his eyes and leaned into her touch.

"Oh, what a sweetie," she told him, and he made a faint whimpering sound in response, though she was pretty sure it was just a sign of pleasure.

"Look at you, Dog Whisperer," Hunter said from behind her, and the dog opened one eye to glare up at him.

"Why don't you go look around and leave me and my buddy here to hang out a bit?" Cookie suggested, continuing to tame the beast with her touch.

Hunter nodded and sidled off without another word. The dog watched him go for a second before returning his full attention to Cookie. She'd never had a dog growing up. Rain had always said they were too much work, and she thought looking after Cookie was quite enough, thank you very much. But Cookie had always liked animals, and it was true that most of them responded to her. Except for that one turtle of Mary Jo Pensky's back in junior high. Who knew turtles didn't like their chins scratched?

After a few minutes, Cookie rose to her feet. The dog head-butted her hand, clearly saying, "Hey, this doesn't mean you have to stop petting me, you know!" Then he took a step and turned so that his entire body was leaning against her legs. He was a big fella, too, so all that weight nearly bowled her over. "Don't worry, I'm not leaving just yet," she told him, patting his head. His tail wagged so energetically it was like someone was thwacking her side with a leather strap. While she petted him she took the opportunity to finally look around properly.

The inside matched the exterior, with its warm and homey feel. There wasn't anything fancy about the tidy, but threadbare place; no high-end electronics, designer furniture, or priceless artwork. But everything had clearly been chosen for comfort and had served its purpose well. It was the home of a nice, working-class couple, not the den of a criminal mastermind, which only confirmed in her mind the fact that Jimmy had been a pawn rather than a crook.

"Hey," Hunter called out from an adjoining room. "Come take a look at this."

Cookie headed toward him, her new best friend trotting along beside her so closely that he constantly brushed against her leg. She liked having him there, she realized. Maybe she should talk to Rain about them getting a dog of their own.

The first room off the living room was a study, dominated by a big, heavy, old, wooden desk. There was also a futon against the far wall under the window, no doubt so that this space could double as a guest room. The center of the desk was littered with papers, while a computer and printer took up the left side, and a large nautical map of the surrounding area had been tacked up on the wall behind it.

Papers rustled as Hunter glanced through them, being careful to use a pen to nudge each one aside. When Cookie reached him, he tapped a page that had been at the bottom of the pile.

She quickly scanned the contents. Her heart got caught in her throat. It was a good-bye and an apology... to his wife.

My Dearest Leslie,

After all the years we spent together, I can't believe I have to write this letter. I'd like to blame it on the cancer, on the healthcare system, on anything other than my own failings, but I can't. What I did was wrong, no matter the circumstances, and I know that. All I can do is offer an explanation. I owe you that much.

All I wanted to do was find a way to pay the outstanding hospital bills and give you that trip to Paris that you so deserve—to spend my final hours living one last adventure with you. But it appears I've gotten in over my head, and now there's no way out. In order to protect you, my love, I won't go into the details here, but chances are, if you're reading this, you need to talk to the police. I'm sorry for what you must be going through, but know I've always loved you and always will.

Your loving husband, Jimmy

"Damn," Cookie muttered, brushing away tears as she finished reading.

"Yeah," Hunter agreed. He pointed to another page in the pile. "He left an updated will, too, more or less."

It wasn't an official document, Cookie saw at once, but just a list of personal items with notes indicating who to give them to after his death.

'My fishing rod and tackle to Larry, as a thank-you for all the times he let me fish off his dock," she read. "My collection of baseball hats to Ed, who could really use something to cover that bald dome of his. My good boots and heavy raingear to Vince, who never can remember to bring his own. My old boots to Buddy'— the dog, who was now sitting at Cookie's feet, barked at that, and she looked down at him. "That's you, huh?" she asked. "Not the most imaginative name, but it suits you." She went back to reading. 'To Buddy, so he can now chew on them to his heart's content and never get yelled at for it.' She had to stop and wipe away more tears.

Considering how advanced his cancer had been, Jimmy had certainly known he didn't have a lot of time left, but this was more than that. This was him realizing he was in real danger from his little side venture and trying to make sure he'd tied up all his loose ends.

"There's this, too," Hunter said softly, indicating a different paper. It was a map, a smaller version of the one on the wall. But this one had been marked up, a circle drawn in part of the water between the island and the open ocean, and dots of color placed within that radius. There weren't any words, but Cookie had a pretty good idea what this was.

"It's got to be his trap locations," she told Hunter. Cookie had spent some time researching the long-held tradition of lobstering one night on the Internet. "These guys, they're super protective of where they drop their traps. Some of them are still using the same spots as their grandpas so it's like family tradition. Since they're inherited, if Jimmy thought he was done for, he'd leave this for Leslie so she'd know where to put them if she kept up the lobstering. Or she could sell the locations to somebody else like you'd cede mining rights when you got too old to keep prospecting yourself."

Hunter frowned. "And if he was using his traps as a way to smuggle drugs—"

"Then this is a map to those drop points." She pulled out her phone.

"It's inadmissible," Hunter reminded her as she aimed the phone's camera at the map.

"I know," Cookie replied. "But we might wind up needing it anyway, and I don't want to count on Leslie doing the right thing and bringing all this in." Her camera snapped as she took the picture, then she tucked her phone away. "We got everything we need?"

"Yeah." Hunter pocketed his pen and strode toward the door.

"Sorry, Buddy," Cookie told the dog, scratching him once more behind the ears. "I've gotta go. You keep an eye out, okay?" He wagged his tail but didn't follow as she left.

It broke her heart to think of him sitting there, waiting for a master who would never return.

15.

THE *GIRLS JUST Wanna Have Fun* ringtone startled Cookie out of her funk. *Leave it to Rain to program the song she considered her anthem into someone else's phone,* Cookie thought. She dug it out of her pocket and lurched forward as it slipped from her fingers, barely catching it before it clattered to the ground.

Hunter let out a low chuckle as she pressed the devise to her ear and said, "Hi, Mom."

"Cookie, come quick!" her mother shouted through the phone. "I've got him!"

"Got who?" she glanced over at Hunter, mouthing the word "Rain" at him. He shook his head in slight exasperation.

"The courier!" Rain replied. "I've got him trapped! But hurry!" Then she hung up.

"She says she's got the courier trapped," Cookie explained as she tucked phone away again and scowled, dreading what they'd find when they got back to the inn. Was her mother really holding the poor man hostage?

"She wants us to hurry."

They'd already been on their way back to the inn, and now resumed that trek, but neither of them upped their pace appreciably. Cookie had been on the receiving end of Rain's melodrama far too many times to fall for it now. Despite her trepidation over what her mother was up to, there was a big difference between the way she'd sounded just now and the way she had when she'd found the hand. Cookie could usually tell the difference, and this wasn't an emergency.

It was clear that Hunter was happy to follow her lead on this. At the same time, Rain didn't lie all that much. She might bend the truth, absolutely, but outright lie? Not often. Which meant she likely had trapped some poor soul. Cookie had a sudden image of her mother straddling some guy, and shuddered as she quickened her pace. If only to save whatever unfortunate man Rain had decided was involved in all this mess.

When they reached the inn, Cookie called out, "Mom? Where are you?" She had her hand on her gun but didn't draw it, and Hunter did the same, his right hand disappearing under his jacket.

She was relieved when her mother called out, "I'm in here, sweetie!" She sounded more excited than anything, and Cookie relaxed a little as she climbed the porch and headed inside.

Rain was waiting for them in the front hall. "What took you so long?" she demanded, but she was grinning ear to ear when she said it. "Well, it doesn't matter," she continued. "He's not going anywhere until I let him."

"Let who, exactly?" Hunter asked, stepping up beside Cookie. "And where is he?"

"Right here," Rain replied. She slid aside to gesture to the small storage space under the stairs. Of course.

Cookie eased her mother out of the way, and with a nod from Hunter, she opened the door.

Her mother's little hippie hideout was exactly the same as it had been when she'd discovered it the other day, except now it was occupied. The courier did match Rain's description, which wasn't surprising at all. If there was one thing her mother knew, after all, it was men. He was tall and slim, with dark hair that curled a bit and came down almost to his shoulders, and he appeared to be in his forties. His eyes could definitely be a warm brown too, but it was impossible to tell right now because they were almost completely closed while his whole body was slack, like he'd been drugged. Which, considering where he was, combined with the skunky odor of the smoke still swirling around him and the joint in his hand, he clearly had.

"Mom, what did you do to him?" Cookie asked as she ducked into the tiny space. Hunter squeezed in behind her, and Rain stayed out by the door, leaning in to talk to them as they gathered around the man, who'd barely reacted to their presence.

"What do you mean?" Rain took a slightly defensive tone, and Cookie glanced back to see that her mother's hands had gone to her hips, her chin lifting defiantly. "I helped out, that's what I did. Just after you left, Hale showed up with another package for you. Since you wanted to question him, I figured I'd better find a way to make sure he stuck around. I offered him some food, but he said he'd already eaten. And my second option, well"—she grinned saucily, tilting her hips and thrusting out her chest—"it would've put him in a receptive frame of mind, for sure, but I doubt you would've appreciated it." She shrugged. "So I went with option three."

"Which was to get him high," Cookie concluded with a sigh. "Mom, you do realize he can't answer a whole lot of questions if he's too stoned to even speak, right?"

"Hey, I can speak just fine," the man in front of her replied, making her jump. His words were slurred, and his eyes only drifted open for a second before closing again, but he was coherent, at least. "Whattaya need?"

Rain giggled. "Isn't he cute?" she said. "And did I mention his name? Hale. Hale Morris. Isn't that just perfect? Rain and Hale. We're like a weather report." Apparently Cookie's mother had decided to claim the courier. Cookie almost felt sorry for him.

"Mister Morris," Hunter said, leaning in a little closer and recoiling slightly from the puff of smoke Hale blew at him. "My name is Hunter O'Neil. I'm a Special Agent with the FBI, and I'd like to ask you a few questions." He was frowning, and Cookie knew exactly why. Anything this guy said would be ruled inadmissible, both because he was higher than a kite and because whatever he said as a result wouldn't be considered reliable. Still, they weren't questioning him as a suspect, at least, not yet.

"Hey, man," Hale replied. His eyes flickered again. "FBI, huh? Whoa. I probably shouldn't be smoking this in front of you." He let out a chuckle, then took another hit.

"No. You shouldn't," Hunter replied. "But right now, I'm a lot more interested in obtaining some information. Is that all right with you?"

Hale nodded, eyes at half-mast. "Sure, ask whatever you'd like. It's cool." He had a nice voice, Cookie thought. Friendly. She could see why her mother would like him.

"Who sent me that package the other day?" Cookie asked, focusing back on the task at hand. "And the one tonight," she added, remembering what her mother had said. She glanced behind her, and as if reading her mind Rain held out a second package, this one only a padded envelope. Cookie was relieved to see that it appeared to be unopened.

Unfortunately, Hale shrugged, as she'd half-expected. "No idea," he replied slowly, lifting his head a little before slumping back again. "Sorry. The office called and said they had a package. All I did was deliver it. That's about it."

"You said the office had the package. That means you didn't go pick it up from the sender, right?" Frustration coiled in Cookie's gut. Whoever was behind this was doing due diligence to not leave any tracks. But one way or another, she and Hunter would find something. They always did.

Hale shook his head, his eyes red and glassy. "Right."

"So, you have no idea who the package is from?" Hunter asked. "There has to be a record of it, and of how they paid for it."

"Yeah, sure," Hale agreed. "The office keeps track of all that stuff. They've got the card on file, probably." He frowned. "Though we do take cash, so it could've been done like that, too."

Cookie felt her shoulders slump. Given how careful the sender had been so far, she was willing to bet he'd done a walk-in with the package and paid in cash. Which meant no tracking him through his credit card, or his email or phone number. And he'd have given a false name, too. Glancing over at Hunter, she could tell by his scowl that he was thinking exactly the same thing. The courier angle was a complete dead end. Which wasn't Hale's fault. He was clearly just doing his job. "Thank you," she told him. Hale nodded, smiling a relaxed, friendly smile that revealed his chipped front tooth. *If Rain could draw, she could have a career as a sketch artist,* Cookie thought. She certainly noticed the details.

Thinking of her mother reminded her of the new piece of evidence. Cookie rose to her feet from where she'd been crouching to talk to Hale and stepped carefully back out of the little space into the hall. The world spun a bit, making Cookie suspect she had a contact high. She sucked in clean oxygen to clear her lungs and held her hand out. Rain turned over the new package without a word. She'd even been holding it in one of their cloth napkins, Cookie noted with approval.

"Hold on," Hunter said, following her out. He shut the door behind him, leaving Hale sprawled on the floor inside. "Allow me." Taking the package from Cookie with one hand, he produced a folding knife from his pocket with the other. The knife was one of those one-hand openers, and he slid out the blade and then used it to slit the package cleanly along one side. That way they avoided destroying any trace evidence the sender might have left, though Cookie wasn't too optimistic. Whoever this was, he or she appeared to be too careful.

Using the napkin, Cookie took the now-open package back and parted its sides to peer inside. No body parts this time, she was relieved to see. Nothing but a folded-up piece of paper. She unfolded it and read: *Tomorrow, 2pm. Come alone.* There was a string of numbers below that Cookie immediately recognized as GPS coordinates.

"All right, so we've got a meet scheduled." Hunter already had his phone out, and was entering the coordinates. "And it's for tomorrow afternoon—here." The screen displayed a map, and Cookie saw Secret Seal Isle and the mainland before it zoomed in on a tiny speck out in the water.

"Great," she muttered. "Another little-bitty island. What'd I do to deserve this?"

"We need to scout it out," Hunter suggested. "Figure out if there's anywhere I can set up to keep an eye on you when you go." He motioned toward the front window. "First thing in the morning," he added after a second. "Too dark to deal with it now."

"Right." Cookie mulled over the logistics. They needed some way to get to the island. The obvious solution was staring her in the face, and though it wasn't her first choice, she didn't see any way around it. "I'll call Dylan," she said finally, fully expecting Hunter's scowl in reply. "We can borrow his boat."

But Hunter shook his head. "Don't worry about that," he told her and smirked a little. "I've got a better idea."

16.

COOKIE WAS AWAKENED the next morning by a rapping on her bedroom door. "If that's a raven, you can just find somebody else to pester," she muttered, lifting her head blearily from her pillow. When the knocking continued, she glanced at her alarm clock to see it was well before five am. She mustered enough energy to shout, "What?"

"Rise and shine," Hunter called out. "Time's a-wastin'."

Grumbling, Cookie dragged herself out of bed and staggered to the door. She threw it open, surprising Hunter, who had his hand already raised to knock again. "Do it and I'll start knocking back on various body parts that really won't enjoy the attention," she warned.

"Fair enough," he replied with a cocky grin. "It got the job done, anyway." He eyed her oversized T-shirt and boy shorts. "I assume you're going to change before we go?"

"I assume you're going to stop being such a pain, but

I keep being disappointed," she shot back, which only earned her a bigger grin. *Why is it guys think it's so adorable when women are snarky at them?* Cookie wondered. Not that she was complaining, She enjoyed busting his…ah, manbits every now and again.

"You might want to wear some sort of disguise," he told her as he turned and headed for the stairs. "In case they're watching the location already."

"Sure, I'll just drag out that nun outfit I've been saving for a rainy day," she retorted, but Hunter just chuckled and waved as he started downstairs.

She took a quick shower, wrestled her hair into a thick braid, and then threw on a bikini top and some jeans cut-offs. Slipping her feet into her sandals, she paused before returning to her closet to rummage around in a box of things they'd found when they'd moved in. "Aha!" she declared, pulling free a large, floppy straw hat and a pair of big, cheesy pink sunglasses. "Perfect!"

On her way downstairs, she had another thought. When she reached the first floor, instead of heading into the sitting room and through to the dining room, Cookie turned right and ducked into her mother's room. Rain had…interesting taste in clothes, and Cookie vaguely remembered seeing her wear something once that might fit the bill here. Sure enough, in Rain's closet she found the exact item she wanted. It was long enough to cover her sufficiently, too, despite her being almost a head taller than Rain and a good deal broader and bustier. Once suitably attired, she made for the dining room.

"Well?" she declared as she entered and stopped in the doorway to strike a dramatic pose. "What do you think? They'll never recognize me, right?"

Hunter was seated at the table, sipping his coffee, and nearly did a spit-take when he saw her. "What the hell is that?" he asked once he'd recovered. "And do you need help getting away from it?"

"It's a beach cover-up," Cookie answered, covering the rest of the distance to the table and plopping into her chair to pour her own coffee and snag a muffin off the plate. "It's what you wear when you don't want to get your swimsuit all dirty or risk having pervs stare at you as if they've never seen a half-naked woman before."

"Sure, if you're Ethel Merman, maybe," Hunter replied, taking a gulp of his coffee. "Or maybe Liberace."

He had a point. Most beach cover-ups were sheer, silky things, like a cross between a sleep shirt and a negligee. This one was more like a casual dress, with a wild flower pattern blazoned across it in colors so bright one needed sunglasses to look at it. On Cookie it fell well below the knees. On Rain it had come down to her feet.

"You said wear something so they wouldn't recognize me," Cookie pointed out. "Nobody's going to recognize me in this."

Hunter shook his head, but he couldn't argue that one and they both knew it.

She grinned, please to win this round. He ignored her as they finished their breakfast in silence, then they hopped in his car and drove down to the docks.

"So, how're we getting out there if we're not borrowing Dylan's boat?" Cookie asked once they'd parked and stepped out, the salt in the air hitting them like a body blow.

Hunter flashed her a conspiratorial smile and led her away from the main ferry dock and toward the smaller, private slips. They passed Dylan's boat, and Cookie knew her former partner recognized it because he stiffened slightly and increased his pace. He didn't stop until they reached a boat in one of the farthest slips.

It was quite a boat, too. Long and sleek, with black sides, it had a short white canopy, a row of black outboard motors, and comfortable couches built into recessed seating areas at both the bow and stern. Cookie recognized it at once.

"What's this doing here?" she demanded as Hunter took a long stride to clear the boat's lip and step onboard. "I thought it would've been impounded, or sold, or something."

This boat had been the site of a death. An accidental one, as it had turned out, but she and Dylan hadn't known that when they'd found it floating on the water with a naked, dead Dickie Dungworth onboard.

Hunter's smile grew. "Since the case was closed and there wasn't a crime, the boat got released back to Dickie's next of kin," he explained. "Hayley didn't have any need for it, so she left it here since the slip's already paid for through the end of the year. I called her last night to see if we could borrow it, and she said absolutely."

Cookie eyed him, one eyebrow raised. "You *called* her and asked to borrow her boat?" she asked, her tone sharper than she'd intended. "I see. And this phone-calling, is this a frequent thing?"

"Wouldn't you like to know," he said, grinning. Cookie had to turn away so he wouldn't see her grinding her teeth in response.

Because, as it turned out, she really would like to know. They'd met Hayley Holloway when she'd turned up to deal with her brother's death and the blackmail plot he'd been handling for her. And when Hunter had come out to join the investigation, he and the famous singer had certainly hit it off. The last time Cookie had seen either of them, they'd been flying back to Philly together on Hayley's private jet. Hunter hadn't said a word about what had happened between the two of them, and Cookie hadn't asked. It was none of her business, after all. She and Hunter were just friends and former partners. If he wanted to go have a meaningless, mindless, brainless fling with some gorgeous, rich, famous popstar, well, good for him.

Only that didn't explain the nausea Cookie felt every time she thought about Hunter and Hayley together. Which was ridiculous, she told herself. She'd made this choice. Hunter had come onto her, more than once, in fact, and she'd told him straight-out that she wasn't interested. But it seemed like certain parts of her hadn't gotten that message.

"We good?" he asked, dropping the grin and stepping just a little closer to her, his eyes finding hers.

"Of course," she replied, because what else could she say? Raising her chin, she forced a little more conviction into her voice. "Yeah, sure, we're good." Then she swatted him on the arm. "Let's get this show on the road, cowboy."

He shook his head at her change in attitude but complied, making his way toward the streamlined cockpit. But once he was there, he paused and began fumbling with his loose running pants.

"Whoa, there," Cookie warned, hurrying over. "When I said 'show,' I didn't mean peepshow, you know." Not that she'd object to Hunter baring his sleek, muscular body, really. But now was hardly the time or the place.

He barked out a laugh as he yanked down his pants to reveal the board shorts underneath. "Figured I should dress appropriately, too," he explained, tugging the pants the rest of the way off and wadding them up before tossing them onto the seat behind him. Now, wearing a tank top, board shorts, and mirrored sunglasses, he really did look like the kind of guy you'd see out for a pleasure cruise on a fancy speedboat like this one.

"Fine," Cookie said, turning away from the sight of him, which was making her pulse race a lot more than it should, "but if you try showing me your bow, I'm out of here." When she and Dylan had found Dickie, the only thing he'd been wearing was a bow tied around his junk.

That got another laugh out of Hunter. "Where're

you going to go, exactly?" he asked as he flipped a switch on the console and the motors roared to life. "We're about to be out on the water, just the two of us, with nobody else for miles around." The smile he gave her was pure sex and sent a dangerous thrill through her... one she was determined to ignore.

"I can always jump overboard and swim back," she replied. "And don't think I won't if you try anything."

But would I really? She couldn't help but wonder. *Or would I go along with it?* Just the thought made her feel like she was betraying Dylan. Not that they'd made any commitments to each other. She and Dylan had only just started...whatever it was they were doing. They hadn't even managed a complete date yet, for heaven's sake. And she'd known Hunter a lot longer, at least as a partner and friend.

This should not be this complicated, Cookie thought angrily. She made her way to the front seating area and flopped onto the forward-facing couch so that her back was to Hunter. She stared out over the water as he maneuvered the cigarette boat away from the dock and out toward the sea. Right now she would've loved to get another mysterious note, a second body part, anything that could distract her from the guy behind her and the other guy somewhere on the island they were rapidly leaving in their wake.

When it came to a choice between solving a crime or dealing with romantic troubles, Cookie would take a good old-fashioned murder and drug smuggling case any day.

17.

"WE SHOULD BE coming up on it," Hunter declared from the captain's chair. They'd been on the water for almost an hour, and Cookie had enjoyed the time to herself, just watching the waves slide past beneath them. She roused herself, though, and abandoned the couch to join him under the canopy. He had his phone out and the GPS up, and was using that to track their position. Sure enough, it showed their current location as almost on top of the coordinates she'd been given.

She turned and scanned the sky and the ocean, glad that her big sunglasses and floppy hat protected her from the glare. "There," she said after a few seconds, pointing. "What's that?"

Hunter frowned as he stared where she'd indicated. "Looks like land," he agreed. "That's got to be it."

Nudging the wheel just a little, he brought the boat around so its nose pointed straight at the dot Cookie had spotted. With all the engines running at full, the boat leaped across the waves, and the dot rapidly grew larger, resolving into a tiny island that was really little more than a large rock jutting up through the water. Its top looked like it had been leveled, however, and Cookie caught sight of something poking out from the other side. "Is that a dock?" she asked.

Hunter threw her a quick sideways smile. "You always did have better eyes than me." She smiled back and tried not to let on how much the rare compliment flustered her.

When they swung around the tiny island, they found that a small portion had been chiseled or blasted out to create a small stone dock. The heavy iron mooring hooks sunk in along the edges left no doubt that its shape was intentional.

Hunter managed to nudge the boat up against the dock, kill the engines, and toss the rope around a hook with only a little fumbling and a few minor bumps that jolted the boat. Cookie decided it was best not to rib him about those. He'd done about as well as she had the last time she'd piloted a boat, and Dylan's was a lot easier to manage than this beast. Instead she just stood there, waiting impatiently until they were securely tied and she could step out onto the dock.

"Clever design," she commented as Hunter's feet thumped on the wood beside her. "It's got an overhang that keeps it out of the sun and out of sight from above."

"What, you think this is some kind of old smuggler's cove?" he asked her, looking around. She noticed that his hand strayed toward the back of his board shorts where his gun was holstered. She'd brought hers as well, and carried it in much the same place, though with the beach dress she wasn't sure she could actually draw it quickly.

Fortunately, she didn't think matters would come to that... at least not during the scouting mission. "Maybe at first," she agreed with his assessment, "but that would've been a long time ago, and I doubt most of this was in place back then." She patted the wall with one hand. It was old, and rough, but it had been hewn carefully, which just further confirmed what she'd already suspected once she'd seen the island's top and this dock.

"What aren't you telling me?" Hunter asked, impatience coloring his tone.

Cookie laughed at him. She'd forgotten how much he hated it when anyone knew something he didn't. "Don't get all bent out of shape," she said. "It's not some big dark secret. Come on, I'll show you." And she led the way up the dock.

The path actually cut right up through the rock in the form of a wide staircase, its steps still almost perfectly level and their edges sharp enough to cut. They could see bright sunlight at the top, and climbed the steps to before emerging on the island's summit.

It was a semicircular space a dozen or so feet across where the stone had been cut, smoothed, and polished with time, with a deep hole at its center. Just in front of that rose a short wall, that had a circular curve to it. Past the wall's upper lip, which dipped outward, the natural stone had been allowed to remain unchanged.

"I give up," Hunter said after pacing out the entire space. "What the hell am I looking at here?"

"It's an old naval battery," Cookie answered. "This is where the big gun was placed. See? It was set into the ground right there." She pointed at the hole. "And it rose up above this wall so it could fire out at anyone trying to attack the coastline."

Hunter looked around, studying the place again, then gave her a penetrating stare. "How did you know that?" he asked, his eyes pinched. "Did Dylan tell you?"

"What, you think I need some guy to educate me on every little thing?" she shot back, annoyed at the implication. "No, Dylan didn't tell me. There's a naval museum on Secret Seal, for your information. When I was exploring during our first week there, I checked it out. There're some pictures of naval batteries and a short explanation of their history and use. Most of them were decommissioned after World War II." She waved at their surroundings. "This has to be one of those, it looks just like some of those pictures."

Hunter nodded. "Right," he said after a second. "I didn't mean to imply anything. I was just surprised, you being a city girl and all. You don't find many of these in Philly."

She knew exactly what he'd been implying, but she decided to let it go and smirked at him. "Yeah, well, the sooner you realize I'm smarter than you, the easier this'll be."

It wasn't the first time she'd said those exact same words to him, or even the second. And their partnership had definitely improved, as had their success rate, when he'd accepted that Cookie wasn't some dumb bunny he needed to protect, but a smart, resourceful partner who brought plenty of her own strengths to the table.

"Okay, okay, point taken," he told her with a chuckle, raising his hands in surrender. Then he scanned the top of the island again. "It's a smart place for a meet," he conceded. "Isolated, easy to control, great sight lines. You set up shop up here, and there's no way anybody's sneaking up on you unless they've got a stealth sub."

"If they did, it'd have to be the James Bond variety," Cookie added. "It's too shallow here for a real sub to get through." The look Hunter shot her said he was impressed, and she had to admit that she was, too. When had she become such an expert on water and islands and ships? Evidently, she'd absorbed a lot more in her time here than she'd realized.

"They set the meet for two p.m.," she recalled, getting back on track. "We could come out here at noon, set up, and turn the tables, catching them on the way in." It was only a little past seven-thirty now, which meant they still had time to run back, get any gear they needed, and then return.

But Hunter shook his head. "We have no idea how early they'll decide to settle in," he pointed out. "They could be on their way right now." He frowned. "Or even holed up somewhere nearby, watching this place." Both of them scanned the surrounding water, but this was the only island in sight. If the drug smugglers were watching, they were doing so from a long distance away with some mighty high-powered binoculars. Still, Cookie ducked down a little, just in case.

"So what're we thinking, then?" she asked. "They want me to come alone, and there's no place for you to hide that's not at least twenty minutes away."

"I know." He rubbed his jaw. "I could borrow a high-powered rifle from the sheriff, maybe, but I'd still need to be close enough for it to do any good. And there isn't any cover anywhere." He growled and pounded a fist on the short wall. "They really did pick the perfect spot."

Cookie sighed. "Maybe we'll think of something on the way back." Pulling out her phone, she snapped photos of the island so they could refer to them later. Then she led the way back toward the stairs and down to the boat. "Home, Jeeves," she ordered as she stepped aboard again and settled back onto the front couch.

"As you command," Hunter joked, casting off the ropes and pushing them away from the dock. Once the boat was free from the island and floating on the waves, he switched on the engines and turned them back toward home. Cookie's home, at least.

Neither of them said anything for a few minutes. Cookie was studying the ocean again, but she was barely paying attention. Instead, her mind was still back on the island, examining it from every angle, looking for a place they could hide. And she kept coming up empty.

It was Hunter's cursing that drew her back to the present first. Then she noticed they seemed to be slowing down. And finally she realized that she could no longer hear the deep, powerful thrum of the boat's many motors all working together to propel the craft forward.

"What's wrong?" she asked, standing and glancing back at him. When she saw him scowling and pounding on the console, she hurried over. "Hunter, what's wrong?"

The face he lifted toward her was half-angry, half-chagrined, like he was both pissed about not having planned better and embarrassed at having to own up to his mistake. "We're out of gas," he finally muttered, not meeting her eyes.

"What? Are you kidding me?" Cookie shoved him out of the way and studied the console. It was fairly straightforward, designed for a rich kid with more money than sense, and the fuel gauge was nice and prominent. As was the needle on it, which was all the way at the E. "How the hell did that happen?" she demanded, rounding on him. "Didn't you check the fuel before we left?"

"Obviously not," he replied, still not looking up. "Sorry."

"Sorry? Sorry? We're stuck in the middle of the bloody ocean because you didn't get gas, and all you can say is sorry?" She smacked him on the shoulder. "What the hell, Hunter? What are we, amateurs?"

"I might've been a little distracted," he admitted, just the hint of a smile tugging at his lips. "I couldn't stop wondering what you had on under that cover-up." He reached out to tug on one of her sleeves, but she slapped his hand away. Trying to be all adorable and sexy was definitely not going to save him now.

"Whatever it is, you're sure as hell not going to find out," she said, and he slumped, looking like a little boy who'd just been told he wasn't getting dessert. She refused to acknowledge how appealing that type of vulnerability was on the man who was normally so cocksure.

With a sigh, Cookie pulled out her phone and searched her contacts. "You know who I have to call now, right?" she said as she hit Send.

"Don't rub it in." Hunter groaned, turning away from her completely.

"Hey, Dylan," she said when he answered. "Listen, I hate to ask this, but is there any way you can come out and give us a lift back in your boat? We went out to check on something, and big, brave Hunter forgot to see if there was enough gas for the voyage home."

"Sure," Dylan replied, and she could tell from the hitch in his voice that he was trying to keep from laughing. It was kind of him, especially considering how well he and Hunter got along, which was not at all. "Text me your coordinates. I'll head out right now."

"Thanks." She hung up and copied their current location from Hunter's GPS into her text. Dylan confirmed he'd gotten it a second later.

"So, Dylan to the rescue, then?" Hunter asked over his shoulder. "Great."

"It's your own damn fault," Cookie reminded him.

"I know, I know." He turned back around slowly, a smile beginning to spread across his face. Evidently, he was over his shame already. "So, what should we do while we wait?"

"I am going to go sit back down and enjoy the sun and the waves and try to forget about how you stranded us out here," she told him. "You should probably sit here by yourself and think about what a dumbass you were, and how you can try not being one in future."

"We could do that," he replied slowly, taking a step toward her. His hands drifted toward the waistband of his shorts. "Or I could show you my bow."

Cookie let loose a smirk of her own as she sank into a combat crouch and raised her hands. "You could try it," she said. "And I'll show you my Krav Maga. How's that for a fair trade?"

"You take all the fun out of life, you know that?" Hunter groused. But his hands fell to his sides, and his shorts stayed on. After a second, Cookie straightened and stalked away. She wasn't actually one-hundred-percent sure she'd have attacked him if he'd stripped in front of her, but she was irritated enough that she might have, and no matter what, it would have complicated things.

It was safer to just sit separately and both fume, if for different reasons.

Safer, but incredibly frustrating. In more ways than one.

18.

HALF AN HOUR later, the steady thrum of a motor alerted Cookie that they were about to have company. She'd been half-dozing on the couch, and now she sat up and peered toward the approaching noise to discover it was Dylan.

And he wasn't alone.

"Scarlett?" Cookie called out as the little motorboat pulled up beside them, Dylan expertly maneuvering so the two boats barely nudged one another. Her best friend waved, and then stepped across to the larger boat. As always, Scarlett looked like a model, perfectly put together in a bikini, cheerful shorts, and a beach cover-up of the more standard—and more attractive—variety. Even her hat and sunglasses were like more refined versions of Cookie's, and not for the first time, Cookie felt slightly awkward and unattractive beside her stylish friend.

Fortunately, Scarlett's easy manner and obvious affection put her at ease again, like always. "Hey, CJ!"

she declared, giving Cookie a tight hug. "I thought I'd pop up for a quick visit, see how the other half lived and all that."

Cookie grinned at her friend. "I love your impromptu trips. But how did you end up out here?"

"Well, I got in late last night and was sleeping when you left this morning. I'd been hanging out at the inn waiting for you to return, enjoying the view." She cast a sly smile in Dylan's direction. "He was working on the roof. And since you were taking forever, I convinced him to take a break and come be sociable." She waggled her eyebrows, because of course she wouldn't pass up the chance to flirt with a guy as hot as Dylan, even if it was completely harmless. "Then he got your call, and I thought I'd tag along." She held out her arms, a huge grin on her face. "Surprise!"

Cookie couldn't help but laugh. "It's always great to see you, Scar," she said, and meant every word of it. "And thank you for coming to get us," she added to Dylan, who'd tied the two boats together and joined them on the larger boat's deck.

"No problem," he replied with that same warm smile that sent a flutter through her every time. He glanced around the cigarette boat again, even though he'd seen it before when he and Cookie had found Dickie dead on the deck. "Still a nice boat," he commented. "Overpowered, though. Like maybe somebody's compensating for something." Then he nodded at Hunter, as if noticing him for the first time. "Hunter."

"Dylan." Hunter's jaw was set, and he was scowling hard enough to split rocks as he stomped over to them. "Thanks for coming to get us." He spit each word out like it hurt him, which it probably did, at least as far as his ego was concerned.

For his part, Dylan made a big show of being unconcerned. "No big deal," he said with a shrug and then winked at Cookie. "I always make sure my boat's gassed up and ready to go. You never know when you're going to have to be the knight in shining armor for a damsel in distress."

Ouch, Cookie thought. Talk about a blow to Hunter's ego. As much as she agreed that Hunter deserved a little comeuppance for his mistake, she didn't actually want to see the two guys in her life come to blows so she stepped in between them, both literally and figuratively. "I'm guessing those are for us?" she asked, indicating the gas cans tucked neatly in the front of Dylan's boat, wedged securely between the hull and the forward bench.

"They are," he agreed. "Should be more than enough to get you back safely."

"Get *him* back, you mean," Cookie corrected. "I'm riding with you. If that's okay." She flushed, realizing she'd just invited herself into his boat.

Dylan didn't seem to mind, however. "Always," he told her warmly. Then he laughed. "Don't want to get stuck again, huh?"

"Something like that." In truth, it was partially

because she was still irritated at Hunter but also because Cookie was annoyed at herself and her uncontrollable hormones. The thoughts and feelings she'd had earlier had unsettled her. Right now, she didn't entirely trust herself to ride back with Hunter. Better to go with Dylan, who she liked and who she knew liked her back. Nice and simple, the way it was supposed to be.

"What, you're going to leave me out here all on my own?" Hunter asked. His eyes had shaded to black, a sure sign that his emotions were on overload. "Thanks a lot."

Fortunately, Scarlett intervened. "I'll ride back with you," she offered, slinging one arm around Hunter's shoulder. Since she was nearly as tall as he was, that wasn't as awkward as it could have been, and she had such a relaxed manner that Hunter first looked surprised but then smiled.

"Fine by me," he agreed. "I could use more pleasant company." He smirked at Cookie, but she just rolled her eyes at him. She resisted sticking out her tongue, but only barely.

"No offense," Scarlett added to Dylan. "But I figure it's better if somebody helps him get home safe. And besides, this one's seats look a lot more comfy." She ran her hand along the nearest chair, which was plush leather. Dylan's boat looked particularly battered and dingy beside it.

"I'm sure they are," he agreed, not looking at all insulted. "Let me take care of the gas situation, and then we can all get going." He hopped back into his boat, moving between the two vessels with the ease of someone who's been on the water all his life, and began pulling the gas cans from the bungee cords he'd used to bind them in place.

Scarlett took advantage of the moment to tug Cookie to one side. "You okay?" she asked quietly. "Your mom said something about a severed hand and some creepy notes?"

Cookie nodded. "I'll fill you in later," she promised, "but we're talking drug smuggling in a big way, and murder on top of that. I'm fine, though. You?" She eyed her friend carefully. "You don't usually pull a surprise visit unless you think I'm in trouble or you desperately need a change of scenery."

Her best friend laughed. "Yeah, well, there may be a guy back home I'm avoiding right now," she admitted. "We had a few laughs, everything was fine, but then he had to go and get all dreamy and dopey on me. So I'm giving him a little space for a few days." She shrugged. "When I get back, we'll see if he can still handle no-strings-attached. If not, I'll have to cut him loose."

Cookie had seen Scarlett with plenty of guys over the years. Neither of the two women had ever had any trouble attracting male companionship. But she'd only seen her friend fall for someone once. It had ended badly, and Scarlett had vowed to never get fooled like that again. Which was both sad and funny, considering what a romantic she was, but she always said it was safer to watch other people fall in love than to ever risk that again herself.

"Well, you know you're always welcome," Cookie assured her, hugging Scarlett again. "Mi casa es su casa."

"Just as long as su clothes aren't mi clothes," Scarlett retorted, tugging one sleeve of Cookie's cover-up. "Where exactly did you get this hideous thing, a refugee from the fifties? A circus performer? And how soon can we burn it?"

"It's Rain's," Cookie answered, laughing. "Hunter thought it'd be better if I had some kind of disguise, just in case."

"It worked," Scarlett informed her. "Nobody'd ever guess it was you under that. At least, I really hope not, otherwise I might not be able to be seen with you anymore."

Cookie put on a mock pout. "You'd let a little thing like poor fashion come between us?" she joked, and Scarlett pretended to seriously consider the question. They were both giggling when Dylan rejoined them.

"All set," he declared. "Shall we?" He offered Cookie his arm like they were off to attend a fancy ball, which just served to send both women into another fit of giggling.

"Don't worry," Hunter called out as Cookie stepped down into Dylan's boat and settled onto the bench there. "I'll take good care of your friend." He made a point of leering at Scarlett.

"I can take care of myself, thank you very much,"

Scarlett told him firmly, hands on her hips. "And Cookie's not the only one who took self-defense classes, so don't get any ideas." The look she shot at Cookie said that Scarlett wouldn't actually object if Hunter did try putting the moves on her, but also that she wasn't about to let him know that. Cookie grinned. Her best friend was an expert on keeping men from getting too full of themselves.

"Just don't let him show you his bow, whatever you do," Cookie warned as Dylan took his seat and started the motor again. He looked at her funny, like he wasn't sure if he should laugh or be worried.

"Is he considering pulling a Dickie?" he asked, shaking his head.

"God, I hope not," she replied, grinning at him.

Meanwhile, up on the cigarette boat, Scarlett was nodding like this was all very important. "No bows, got it," she announced, giving Cookie a big thumbs-up. "I don't care how *big* they might be." That and the wink she added told Cookie she had indeed remembered the story about Dickie and his ribbon, and knew what Cookie had meant.

Cookie was still laughing as Dylan gave his boat some gas and pulled it away from the other vessel, leaving Scarlett and Hunter behind.

19.

"DO I WANT to know what you two were doing out there?" Dylan asked as he piloted them back toward the island. He had his face turned away from her as he spoke, but Cookie could tell by his tone that his expression was bleak at best.

"Checking out a lead on the case," she answered. Then she caught herself. He'd been with her when she'd found the drugs, and again when the hand had arrived, so why was she keeping details from him now? "I got another package," she added instead, though revealing information felt like pulling her own teeth. "No body parts this time, just a note. With coordinates."

Now he did glance at her, and although his jaw was still set she could see that his eyes were that familiar warm blue she found so enticing, not the steel-gray they turned when he was upset. "Let me guess," he offered, "they led you out to the old naval battery?" She must have gaped at him, because he chuckled. "It's the only thing for miles around," he explained. "Good spot for a meet, especially if you don't want any surprises."

"That was my thought, too," she agreed, pleased that he didn't seem angry with her anymore. She hadn't been sure how he'd take the fact that she and Hunter had been gallivanting about together… even if it was because of the case. "There's no place to set up, no place to keep watch without being seen ourselves." She banged one hand on the bench beside her. "I'd be infinitely happier if these guys were a lot less competent."

Dylan nodded. "You could use a drone," he suggested after a second. "One of those little ones you can buy over the counter. They come with cameras, most of them, and they've got a decent range. You should be able to set up on one of the other little islands out here and use that to at least get a glimpse of who's out here and what they've got waiting for you."

"Oh." Cookie started to smile, but that suddenly switched to a frown followed by a whole string of curses.

"Whoa!" Dylan looked surprised. "Was it something I said?"

"Yeah… no… yeah." She sighed. "It's a smart move, thanks. The only problem is, these guys…"

"Have been playing it smart the whole way," he finished for her, his expression now matching her own. "Crap."

"Exactly." She squinted up at the sky, checking their surroundings. "I don't see anything right now, but that doesn't mean they weren't out here before. Between the water and the wind, I'm not sure I would've heard something as small as a drone, so they easily could've seen us over there checking it out."

He nodded. He also didn't try to tell her everything would be fine, or that she was just worrying needlessly, which she appreciated. She'd rather have honesty than platitudes any day.

"Would it matter if they did see you?" he finally asked. "I mean, when were you supposed to meet them there?"

"Two o'clock." She checked her watch. That was still a few hours away.

"So maybe it doesn't even matter," Dylan suggested. "I'm guessing you're supposed to show up alone at two?" Cookie nodded. "But the note didn't say 'don't go anywhere near there beforehand,' right?" He shrugged. "Makes sense to me that you'd scout it out. Maybe it will to them, too."

"Maybe," said Cookie, but she wasn't so sure. These guys weren't exactly the kind to deal fairly. They wanted to hold all the cards, and they were willing to kill to do that. People like that might easily view her going anywhere near the island before the meet as disobeying orders.

And with people like that, disobeying always brought consequences.

They didn't talk much the rest of the way back. Cookie was wrapped up in her own thoughts, and Dylan seemed to understand she needed the space. Hunter and Scarlett were right behind them in the cigarette boat.

Cookie was surprised Hunter hadn't just zoomed past them, but she figured he was rationing his limited gas supply. Having to endure Dylan bailing him out twice would be entirely too much for his inflated alpha-male ego.

Hunter was tossing the mooring rope around one of the dock cleats when Dylan and Cookie walked down the pier to meet him and Scarlett, the dock hinges squeaking with the movement of their steps. The four of them then headed back up toward the inn in Hunter's car.

Along the way, Cookie shared Dylan's idea about the drones with Hunter. Scarlett listened in, of course, which was fine—Cookie didn't have any secrets from her, and wasn't about to start now.

"Damn, wish I'd thought of that," Hunter said. He nodded grudgingly at Dylan, who was trying not to smirk. "You're right, that would work." Then he scowled. "And yeah, they probably figured out the same thing ages ago. Damn."

"So we're assuming they saw you guys there, right?" Scarlett asked. "But so what? As long as Cookie goes to the actual meet alone, it shouldn't change anything."

Dylan favored her with a smile. "That's what I said." He held up his hand, and Scarlett high-fived him. Cookie laughed at that, not sure if she should be happy or suspicious that her best friend and the guy she was maybe-almost-sort of dating were getting along so well.

They'd just reached the top of the hill where the inn

came into view, when Dylan frowned. "What's that?" he asked, his voice shifting instantly from friendly banter to deadly serious. Cookie and the others all glanced toward where he was pointing, and saw something small and bright crumpled on the ground up ahead.

Hunter stopped the car and managed to get to it first, using long strides to cover the distance. He had only just scooped it up when Cookie reached him, and he held it out to her. It was a long, gauzy scarf, its bright tie-dye standing out even in the midday sun. Cookie recognized it at once.

"That's Rain's," she said, accepting it from Hunter. She was winding it about her hand when she noticed something else. "And so are those." She hurried over to the bejeweled flip-flops and snatched them up as well.

"I've got a pair of sunglasses over here," Scarlett said from a few paces farther on.

"And, um, pretty sure that's the top she was wearing this morning," Hunter added in a strangled voice, indicating another article of clothing that had been tossed upon the ground.

"Mother!" Cookie growled, piling each item in her arms as the others brought them to her. Dylan shame-facedly handed over a pair of jean shorts that Cookie knew for a fact barely covered Rain's butt, but Scarlett was laughing when she turned in a lacy bra.

"Looks like somebody's getting busy around here," she commented as she contributed the lingerie to the pile.

"She's always *busy*," Cookie fumed, "and I bet I know exactly where, too." She stormed around the house to the shed built against its side wall. This was where she'd caught Rain once before, "entertaining" a local fisherman named Anthony. And, true to form, Rain had thought it was hilarious that Cookie and Hunter had walked in on them. Which was why Cookie made sure she was well ahead of him when she reached the shed and threw the doors open so hard they shook.

"All right, Mother, this has really—" she started, but stopped mid-rant as her brain caught up with what her eyes had already told her. The shed was empty.

"Should we be seeing something other than some lawn equipment?" Scarlett asked, peering over her shoulder.

"Yeah, a naked Rain and a willing male victim," Cookie replied. She stepped back and shut the shed again. "They can't have gotten far—not without all this." She tried to shove away the sudden mental image of Rain streaking through town and concentrated on her present surroundings instead. "Mom!" she shouted. "Where are you?"

Hunter, Dylan, and Scarlett all joined her, both in shouting and in checking around the inn. But their search came up empty. And the longer they went without locating Rain, the more Cookie started to worry that this wasn't one of her mother's little dalliances after all.

When her phone chirped, she nearly dropped the

bundle of clothing she'd been carrying. Instead she juggled it so she could get to her phone and check the screen. There was a text from an unknown number.

Cookie clicked on it, and gasped. The others were at her side in an instant. The photo wasn't very good, only a head shot, but even blurry it was still very obviously Rain's terrified face.

Below the picture the text read, *Why can't women ever follow directions?* Then another line appeared. *Let's try this again.* And finally: *Tea Tripper. 2pm. Come alone or Rain will fall.*

Heart pounding, Cookie immediately tried calling the number, but no one answered. "Damn it!" she almost hurled her phone across the kitchen where she was standing, but stopped herself just in time. She might need the darn thing, and it wasn't the phone's fault, anyway.

It was hers.

"I should've been here," she muttered, clutching Rain's clothes to her chest. "I shouldn't have been out there, playing cop again. This is my fault. I didn't do what they said, and now they've got her." She gazed up at Hunter, who had put a hand on her back. "What am I going to do?"

"We're going to get her back," he told her stonily, not a hint of doubt or fear showing on his face or in his voice. Which would have been a lot more reassuring if Cookie hadn't already known that he was great at presenting a brave front, even when things were hopeless.

"I mean it, Charlie. We'll get her back safe and sound. I promise."

She nodded. It was what she needed to hear, even though they both knew you could never guarantee something like that. They'd seen hostage situations go sideways way too many times to believe it always worked out okay. But right now, she had to cling to that notion, at least.

"Two o'clock," Dylan said grimly. "That doesn't give us a lot of time. We're going to have to move if we want to make it."

Hunter raised an eyebrow and crossed his arms. "What's this 'we' shit?" he said harshly. "We appreciate the lift back and all, but Charlie and I've got it from here."

"The hell you do," Dylan replied, stepping up and throwing Hunter's hard stare right back at him. "Not only is Cookie my friend, Rain is too. *I'm* going."

"*You're* not," Hunter warned, his eyes going flat black with cold determination. "Even if I have to handcuff you to the porch."

"You're welcome to try," Dylan growled right back, settling into a fighting stance, feet apart, knees slightly bent, hands loose at his sides.

Cookie had been staring at this, and only now did she find her voice. "What the hell is wrong with you two?" she demanded of both of them. "They've got my mom and you're busy waving your dicks at each other? Grow up!"

Both men had startled at her shout, and at least had the decency to look embarrassed now.

"Seriously," Scarlett added, backing Cookie the way she always did. "You two need to get it together right the hell now. Because if these guys are as smart as they sound, it's going to take all three of you to stop them."

Cookie nodded. And after a second, so did Hunter and Dylan. Neither of them said anything, but Cookie could see that they had just declared a temporary truce.

"That shop's got a back door," Dylan offered after a minute. "It backs up on the water and has its own private dock. A lot of the shops over there do."

"Can you get to it without them spotting you?" Cookie asked, glad to have something actionable to focus on.

Dylan's nod was matter-of-fact. "They'll never see me coming," he promised. And Cookie believed him.

"I'll take the front," Hunter declared. He and Dylan exchanged a glance, one of two rivals who had found a common enemy. For now.

Had the drug smugglers not kidnapped her mother, Cookie would almost feel sorry for them. Instead, they deserved whatever they got. "I'll go in first," she declared, and she held up a hand when both men started to protest. "No. If I don't, they'll likely hurt her. I have to look like I'm scared enough to follow their rules. You both wait five minutes and then hit them. That should give me enough time to grab to Rain and get her somewhere safe."

"I don't like it," Hunter told her bluntly. "Five minutes is plenty of time for everything to go to hell, and you'll be alone and unarmed." They both knew there was no way the smugglers would let her through the door with her piece.

But she shrugged. "It's the best chance we've got." None of them challenged her, and she added, "Right, let's go."

They gathered up the drugs in a duffle bag and started back toward Hunter's car, Cookie still holding Rain's clothes. She turned to hand them to Scarlett, which was when she realized that her friend was right there with her. "Where do you think you're going?" she demanded.

"With you," Scarlett replied. "Don't even try it," she said, stopping Cookie before she could get out a single word of protest. "Somebody's got to make sure these two don't kill each other. I'll stay in the boat, I promise. But you know you're not getting rid of me, so save your breath."

Cookie considered arguing, but knew her friend was right. Once Scarlett set her mind to something, that was it. So she hugged her instead, a quick sideways squeeze because they were all still moving. "Thanks."

"Of course." Scarlett grinned at her. "Now let's go kick some ass and get your mom back, okay?"

Walking down the hill with her three friends, Cookie actually felt a spark of hope.

Those smugglers wouldn't know what hit them.

20.

"Y OU SURE ABOUT this?" Hunter asked as they slowed to a stop a block from the Tea Tripper shop. Dylan had dropped them off and was on his way to the dock behind the shop, where Scarlett would stay at Dylan's boat as promised, so it was just the two of them. "It's not too late to call in the cavalry," he pointed out carefully, like someone trying to defuse a bomb without instructions, feeling every inch as carefully as possible. "Sheriff Watkins could be here in minutes."

Cookie snorted at that. "Yeah, great," she replied, "and what would that bring to the table exactly? A grandma with a shotgun and one, maybe two deputies who've probably never even had to draw down on a real live person, let alone been in a gunfight?" She shook her head. "Better to leave this to the professionals." *Even if I'm not one anymore*, she thought but refused to say aloud.

"Well, what about the Bureau, then?" Hunter offered. "If I told Spinner what was going on, he'd have a team in the air in a half hour, tops." Spinner had been their boss back in Philly, and was still Hunter's direct superior.

Cookie said, "No. We don't have that kind of time.

Hunter sighed, resigned. "At least let me go in first," he said instead. "Draw their fire, take a few of them out." Cookie didn't like the fact that he was already assuming it would come to bloodshed, but she couldn't blame him. In a situation like this, against people like this, they had to prepare for the worst. Except the absolute worst would be that they'd already killed their supposed hostage, and Cookie wasn't willing to even entertain that notion yet.

She also wasn't willing to let her former partner get killed... not if she had anything to say about it. Which is why she replied, "It has to be me, remember? You show up in my place, and they'll start shooting before you can get a word in. I can talk them up a bit, stall, look around, give you and Dylan a chance to get into position." She grinned as the familiar rush of adrenaline fueled her confidence. "Then we cut them down."

"Fine," he agreed, clearly not happy but unable to come up with a better plan. "You ready?"

Cookie pulled out her cell phone and texted Dylan that she was about to go in. Then she called Hunter's phone, waited until he'd picked up, and then slid the phone back into her pocket, the call still active. Being able to hear what was going on would give him a little extra edge. She hoped. "Ready."

He reached out and tugged her into a quick hug. "Don't get dead." he said, locking eyes with her.

She smiled at that. "You either." It was what they'd always told each other right before a bust. They bumped fists, and then Cookie turned and walked toward the tea shop. Hunter hung back in case anyone was watching. She knew he'd set his watch to count down five minutes, and that he'd loiter for those minutes trying to look innocuous while staying close enough to barge in when the time was up.

She didn't look back. There wasn't any point. Either they'd both make it through this, one of them would, or neither of them would. But hesitating now could be the deciding factor, and not in a good way. She just had to see it through.

When she pushed the front door open, the wind chimes were just as cheerful sounding as they'd been the other day. But the sign on the door had been turned to Closed, and there weren't any noises inside the shop. "Hello?" she called out as she entered.

"Over here," a man replied.

Cookie followed the sound of his voice through the cluttered aisles to the sales counter. She frowned as she approached, studying the man. He was a dozen or more years her senior, with rust-colored hair and beard, wearing jeans and a flannel work shirt over a T-shirt. He looked familiar.

"I know you, don't I?" she asked. He glanced away, embarrassed, and it was that look of shame and guilt that jogged her memory. "You're the guy from the shed!" she burst out. She recalled the conversation with Rain and Winter right here just the day before. "Anthony."

He squirmed under her scrutiny. "Yeah, look," he started, but Cookie cut him off.

"Where is she?" she demanded. "Where's my mother?"

He still couldn't meet her eyes. "I—I'm really sorry about all this," he finally managed to spit out. "I mean, everything, this whole thing… it wasn't supposed to be like this. It was just to make a little extra cash. Nobody was supposed to get hurt."

"Yeah? Tell that to Jimmy Calder," Cookie snapped, not about to let him off the hook. "Or my mother. Now. Where. Is. She?"

"She's in the kitchen," Anthony answered sheepishly, staring down at his feet. "Back there." He jerked his head toward the beaded curtain that separated the storefront from the café.

Cookie stomped past him without another word. She couldn't see Anthony putting up much of a fight against Hunter. But a small, vicious part of her hoped he would, just so he could get the beatdown he clearly deserved.

The café was empty except for two big, burly guys sitting at the centermost table. They had a plate of cookies between them, mugs of what was probably coffee, and they each had a pistol sitting out on the table in easy reach. Neither of them grabbed for their weapon when she entered, but she caught the faint twitch as they each considered it, shifting just a little so they could face her but still be able to grab and shoot in a heartbeat.

These guys really were good.

"Where are the drugs?" one of them demanded. His eyes zeroed in on the duffle bag she had slung over her shoulder, but Cookie clutched the straps to her.

"Where's my mother?" she replied, staring them down.

For a second she thought the men would insist on seeing the drugs first, but finally the one who'd spoke shrugged. "In the pantry," he answered, nodding at another beaded curtain, this one set in the side wall near the corner. Neither he nor his companion did anything to stop her when she headed in that direction. Their complacency confirmed her first impression—these were the foot soldiers, not the bosses. He, or she, would presumably be waiting inside.

The kitchen was small but professionally outfitted, and surprisingly tidy for Winter. It had built-in cabinets along the two walls on either side, with a door and a window taking up most of the back.

Two large, well-built men leaned against the center island. Their eyes locked on Cookie the minute she came into view. They'd clearly been waiting for her. Like the men outside, their movements were precise and efficient, like they'd had military training. They both wore dark clothing and sunglasses, and the one on the left was actually in a silk suit. *He has to be the boss*, Cookie thought.

Two guns lay on the island in front of them along with an almost-empty tray of pastries. Cookie had a brief flash of hope that the baked goods might be similar to her mother's brownies. Dealing with a bunch of stoned-out-of-their-gourds drug runners would be a whole hell of a lot easier than facing ones who were stone-cold sober. Unfortunately, the men didn't seem any the worse for wear. Pity.

"Where are my drugs?" the one in the suit asked once Cookie stopped just out of his reach. His gaze flicked to the bag but then back to Cookie's face, which meant he was well-trained enough not to let himself get distracted. Damn.

"Where's my mother?" she answered. "She'd better not be hurt."

The two men laughed at that. "No, but a few of my guys have some nasty bruises on account of her," the smuggler replied. "She's a fighter, your ma." He grinned like that was funny or a high compliment. To him it was probably both.

Cookie didn't budge or reply, and after a second the smuggler sighed. At his nod, his companion got up, walked around the island, and headed for the door just to the side of Cookie. She moved out into the kitchen proper, pivoting as she did so she could still keep Mr. Smuggler in sight as his henchman pulled the door open.

The narrow, dark pantry was filled with tall, industrial-style shelves. Tied to the nearest shelf were two women who continued to struggle against their ropes, freezing only when they noticed their new audience.

One of the women was Winter. That made sense, and Cookie wished she'd thought of that. Of course Winter would be here. It was the middle of the day. And since the smugglers obviously knew about her connection to Rain, they must have realized she would make an excellent second hostage.

The other woman was Rain. She was wearing only a towel, and there was duct tape covering her mouth, proof that she'd continued her lifelong trend of never knowing when to shut up. She looked scared but also furious, and her eyes went wide when she caught a glimpse of Cookie.

Then the man shut the pantry door again.

"Now," his boss said quietly and far too calmly for Cookie's liking. "Are we ready to do business?"

21.

"FINE." COOKIE UNSLUNG the bag from her shoulder and tossed it so it landed right at his feet. "There are your drugs. Now let them go."

He didn't lean down, which was what she'd hoped. Instead he nudged the bag open with his foot just enough so that he could see the packages within. After a second, he nodded.

"Good," he said, glancing back up at Cookie. "That is an excellent start. Now where's the rest?"

She frowned at him. "What 'rest'?" she asked. "That's all I have. That's what was in the lobster trap, every kilo of it. I didn't even open the packages." Which was true. She hadn't needed to because she'd known what they contained.

His frown matched her own, but she suspected it looked a whole lot more menacing than hers. "Do not play games," he warned. "I want the rest of my supply. Then you can have your mother and her friend back." He smiled, showing way too many teeth for it to be friendly. "If you act quickly, they may even be un-harmed. Mostly." His sidekick laughed at that, a short, ugly bark that suggested he would enjoy hurting the two women far too much for it to be merely business.

Cookie spread her hands. "No games," she promised. "I don't have anything else. Just what I found in the lobster trap."

Mr. Smuggler banged his fist down on the table, causing the cookie tray to jump. "Enough! Calder set up a dozen drop points for us. This was one. I want the rest. You will bring them to me. Now."

"I don't have even a trace of a clue what you're jabbering about," Cookie insisted, but she had a sinking sensation in her gut that she was actually lying. She flashed back to the map Hunter had found on Calder's desk, the one that showed a bunch of marked spots in the waters around them. She'd already guessed that those were Jimmy's lobster trap locations, and if he was using all of his traps to smuggle drugs, each one of those was a potential drug haul. It sounded like she'd been right. Jimmy had taken a full shipment right before he died. But clearly he hadn't told this guy where each one was placed. He must have farmed out the locations to each intended recipient, one apiece, so he was the only one who knew all of them. Smart. Except now Jimmy was dead and this guy wanted all of his drugs back at once, rather than waiting for each of the designated dealers to find and collect theirs.

And she had a photo of the map with all those

locations marked saved on her phone, right there in her pocket. Her first instinct was to confess, to hand over the phone and the photo, collect Rain and Winter, and be done with it. But the part of her that had been FBI knew better. This guy was moving a large quantity of drugs, more than enough to mean a heavy prison sentence if he got caught. Plus, he was working in a business that often resulted in death or torture or both. And he'd already demonstrated that he had no problem kidnapping innocents, or killing people and chopping up their bodies. She knew he wasn't about to let three witnesses walk out of there alive.

The minute she told him where to find the rest of his drugs, she was dead, and Rain and Winter would be too. Which meant the only thing she could do now was stall for time and hope Dylan and Hunter could take out his men before any innocent people died.

In situations like this, reality blurred and the concept of time seemed to ceased to exist. She felt as if it had been hours since she'd walked in the door, even though she knew it couldn't be more than five minutes. But she had no idea where she was in that countdown.

All she could do was be ready for whenever it hit zero. "Look—" she started, but a sudden banging interrupted her. Only it wasn't coming from outside, or the front room. It was coming from the pantry.

As Cookie turned to stare at the pantry door, there was more banging, some muffled screams and shouts, and then a loud crash. She jumped. So did the two men, both of them reflexively grabbing for their guns.

A loud gunshot sounded from outside, somewhere beyond the back door. At the same time, the front door slammed open, and a second later Cookie heard shouting, more shooting, and then the heavy thud of bodies hitting the floor.

The cavalry had arrived.

Relieved, but knowing better than to let her own guard down, she turned her attention back to the two men sharing the kitchen with her. Mr. Smuggler leaned down to snatch the bag off the floor and tossed it onto his shoulder—the shoulder of his empty hand, she noted with a pang of dismay. At the same time, he gestured toward her with his gun.

"You," he declared, "are coming with us."

His henchman advanced on her, gun in one hand, the other outstretched to grab her by the arm, a nasty grin spreading across his wide features.

Just then the back door slammed open and Dylan came charging into the room. He collided with Mr. Smuggler before he could turn and raise his gun, and the two of them hit the floor so hard that Cookie felt the vibration under her feet. Luckily, the drug dealer took the brunt of the impact.

The henchman stopped and twisted around, clearly trying to decide if he should continue going after Cookie or help his boss.

Cookie solved that dilemma by kicking him in the crotch as hard as she could. He doubled over, his gun clattering to the floor as he clutched at his privates, howling in pain. Hunter was there in a flash and punched the guy in the jaw, temporarily ending his pain by knocking him unconscious.

"You okay?" he asked her, breathing heavily. He had his gun out and looked like he'd been in a fight, but he didn't appear to be harmed.

"I'm fine," Cookie assured both him and Dylan, who had now risen to his feet as well. Mr. Smuggler was still on the ground, out cold, and Dylan appeared uninjured. Now that Cookie had reassured herself about the two of them, her thoughts flew to the loud noises that had echoed from the pantry. "Mom!" she cried, darting for the door.

She yanked it open, and then froze, staring at the sight within. Two chalk-white figures lay on the floor, blinking up at her amid a pile of wrecked shelving, canisters, boxes, and other cooking paraphernalia. Both of them made muted gasping sounds when they saw her.

"Are you okay?" Cookie asked, bending down to free them. Jars, bottles, and boxes lay everywhere, and she had to be careful not to kneel on any of the scattered broken glass. She could already see what must have happened. After the henchman had closed the door on them, Rain and Winter must have started trying to break free again. Instead, their efforts had apparently pulled the entire shelf over, dumping all of its contents on them and the floor around them. That had included a large, open bag of flour—hence the whiteout. They didn't look hurt, though, just a bit stunned.

When Cookie finally managed to free Rain's hands, her mother sat up without any problem, wiping flour off her face. As Cookie turned to help Winter, her mother yanked the duct tape from her own mouth.

Then she screamed.

At first Cookie thought it was just a reaction to the pain, until Rain gasped out, "Cookie, look out!"

Spinning while still in a crouch, Cookie found herself staring at Mr. Smuggler. He'd apparently recovered enough to grab his gun again.

And he had it pointed straight at her.

22.

TIME SEEMED TO slow down.

"No!" Cookie heard Hunter shout. But he was too far away to do anything. So was Dylan. There wasn't anyone between her and the drug smuggler.

Fortunately, Cookie wasn't the type of girl who needed anyone's protection. She reached out, snagging the closest fallen item, realizing only after the fact that it was a jar of homemade preserves, and hurled it at the drug boss's head, fastball-style.

When she'd been a kid, Cookie had been on the neighborhood softball team. She'd been a backup pitcher, and a pinch hitter. The reason she hadn't been the team's main pitcher? She had a tendency to throw at the batters, rather than over the plate.

Apparently she hadn't lost her skill, because the jar flew through the air, slamming full-force into the man's head with a loud crack. He jerked from the impact, his aim going wide as he collapsed on the floor. But his finger still squeezed the trigger, and the echo of the gunshot in the small kitchen was deafening.

Through the noise, Cookie heard a second sound of glass exploding, and felt something splash across her lower torso. Glancing down, she saw that a large, dark red splotch now covered most of her stomach. The overwhelming aroma of raspberries assailed her.

"Charlie!" Hunter threw himself at her, sinking to his knees and grabbing her shoulders. "Hang on!"

"Hang on?" she frowned at him, her brain still catching up with events as her perception of time once again returned to normal. Then she registered his wide eyes and panicked expression and realized what was going on. "Oh! No, I'm fine." She lifted her shirt to show the undamaged skin beneath. "See? It's jam. Raspberry. Raspberry jam."

"What?" For half a second he frowned at her, as if she'd pulled some really mean joke on him. Then his face cleared. And the next thing Cookie knew, she was in his arms.

"I thought—" Hunter mumbled, his face buried in her shoulder, his arms squeezing her tight. "I thought it was—" He clearly couldn't bring himself to finish the thought, even now that he knew it was wrong.

"I know." She patted him on the back, returning his hug as the reality of her near-miss started to sink in. If Mr. Smuggler had gotten his shot off before her toss had connected, or if his aim hadn't strayed, she could have been gut-shot for real. Or even worse. And with the close quarters, the jam, and everything else, she could totally see why Hunter had been so worried.

It also hit her, hard, that she'd never seen him get this worked up before. They'd faced danger together a bunch of times. And they'd seen friends and co-workers get hit, too. Even had a few near misses themselves before. Hunter had always been sympathetic to those who'd been wounded, and angry that good people should be put at risk, but Cookie had never seen him this overwhelmed.

Part of her wondered if it was because she was no longer an active agent or if there was more to it than that. The rest of her was just reveling in the fact that she was still alive. She registered all the little facts of the world around her: the overwhelming aroma of raspberry jam, the thin sheen of sweat coating her limbs from fear and exertion, the strain on her legs from crouching, the flour that still billowed about them, making her eyes itch and her throat scratchy. And Hunter's firm body in her arms, his own powerful limbs wrapped around her warmly, protectively. The scent of cologne and sweat filled her nostrils as his heart beat against her chest.

She was suddenly filled with the urge to kiss him. Twisting her head a fraction of an inch, she found that he was staring at her, their eyes only inches apart, his gaze so warm and welcoming she felt she could fall right into him. His lips were parted slightly. Her own opened in response as she leaned closer, his head inclining as well—

"She all right?" Dylan asked, popping up in her

peripheral vision.

The sight of him jerked Cookie back to reality, to their current predicament, and to her tangled love life. She responded by pulling back from Hunter ever so slightly, but enough that he noticed.

His body stiffened, and after a second he loosened his grip and retreated a step, rising back to his feet and offering her a hand up. His eyes had gone hooded, the emotions she'd seen a second ago vanishing under a black veil as if they'd never existed.

But Cookie was sure she'd seen them there. Just as she was sure her own heart was hammering in response. Her brain was swimming with thoughts that had only been half-formed notions before but now seemed almost painfully sharp.

Taking a deep breath and shaking her head to clear it, she let Hunter pull her to her feet. "I'm fine," she managed, her voice a little shaky as she brushed herself off, the gesture futile against the red jam-and-flour paste now coating her. "I'm going to need the world's longest shower when I get home, though."

Dylan studied her for a second, his eyes dropping down briefly to the stain on her shirt, then nodded and tilted his head toward the front of the shop. "The others are tied up." He slid past her to help Rain and Winter. A short, sharp, black-bladed knife had appeared in his hands, and he made quick work of their bonds before hauling both of them to their feet and out of the pantry. In less than a minute, the five of them were all standing around the kitchen over the bodies of Mr. Smuggler and his henchman, both of whom had been securely tied up.

Rain wasted no time in launching herself at Cookie. "I thought you were dead!" she wailed, clutching Cookie tight. "I thought we were dead!" For once, Cookie didn't think her mother was being overly dramatic.

"It's okay, Mom," Cookie assured her, hugging her back. "We're all okay." Her eyes sought Dylan over Rain's shoulder, but after a quick nod he turned away.

"I'll let Scarlett know it's safe," he said, pulling out his phone.

Cookie felt a twinge of regret at his cool, businesslike demeanor, but told herself it was just him being in ready mode, not anything personal. She wasn't so sure, though. Dylan clearly had a very good poker face, but she thought just for a second when he'd first spotted her and Hunter in the pantry, his eyes had shown a world of hurt instead.

23.

SCARLET JOINED THEM a few minutes later with Rain's clothes in hand. Everyone was still in the kitchen, waiting for Sheriff Watkins to send officers to retrieve the downed smugglers. Winter and Rain were huddled at the table, with Cookie hovering over them, unsure how to play mother and help with their obvious shellshock. Dylan and Hunter were arguing.

"I had three of them—you only had two," Hunter bit out as Scarlett handed Rain her clothing.

"Your three included Anthony, who likely didn't even put up a fight," Dylan countered. "I bet when he saw you burst in he probably just hid behind the counter, hands over his head, shrieking 'don't hurt me!'" The disgusted look that twisted Hunter's face confirmed this analysis, and Dylan nodded. "You also had cover. I didn't. My two were guarding the back door, with a clear line of sight."

"And one of them got a shot off on you," Hunter argued. "I heard it." So had Cookie, she recalled. That was what had startled the boss and his henchman into moving.

"He missed," Dylan replied with a shrug. "And I'm pretty sure I heard shooting in here, too." Had there been? Cookie had a hard time remembering the exact sequence of events.

"Do we need to get out a ruler?" Scarlett asked, sauntering over to the table like she was just meeting the bunch of them for a late lunch. She completely ignored the drug runners tied and gagged on the floor, but Cookie noticed the very faint tremble to her best friend's hand, and the way her lips were tighter than normal. She was clearly working very hard to maintain a casual composure, and Cookie for one appreciated it.

"Excuse me?" Hunter eyed her in confusion.

"Well, with all the dick measuring you two are doing, I just thought it would be faster." Scarlett smirked, and Cookie stifled a laugh.

Dylan had the decency to look properly chastised as he nodded to Cookie and mouthed, "Sorry." Hunter, on the other hand, let out a huff of impatience.

The exchange was interrupted by a loud, businesslike knock on the front door. "Hancock Sheriff!" Sheriff Watkins's familiar voice rang out. "Open up!"

Cookie hopped up and hurried to the front, wiping her mouth with the back of her hand as she went. She wasn't surprised to see the two men in the café tied like the rest, or to find Anthony handcuffed but conscious and ungagged in the front room behind the counter. It looked like Dylan had been right on the money, there.

Sheriff Watkins eyed her closely when Cookie opened the door. "Everyone all right?" the sheriff asked. She had a half dozen men behind her. Cookie hadn't even realized the Hancock department had that many deputies, and she wondered if some of them had been called in just for this.

"We're all fine, thank you," Cookie answered, stepping back and swinging the door wider so the sheriff and her men could enter. "We've got seven for you, all but one unconscious. He's in here, there are two in the next room, two in the kitchen, and two out back."

Watkins nodded and gestured at two of the men. "Go get the ones out back," she instructed, and they peeled off. Cookie realized belatedly that they were wearing firefighting gear. That explained the large numbers.

They paused at the counter, and Watkins glared down at Anthony with that stern, grandmotherly look of hers. "Doesn't look like a hardened drug smuggler," she muttered, and Anthony paled.

"He's a local," Cookie answered for him. "Anthony something, I don't know the last name. I'm guessing he got roped into helping them the same way Jimmy Calder did." At the mention of Jimmy, Anthony's face paled, and he looked like he was going to be sick.

"Hmph. Well, if he doesn't have a record and is willing to play ball, we might be able to cut him a deal," Watkins offered, clearly for the lobsterman's benefit. The way his eyes widened, Cookie had a feeling he was eager to cooperate. Which was good, because she doubted they'd get much out of the others.

Watkins detailed one man to escort Anthony back to the station, and the rest followed her and Cookie into the café, where two more stopped to take those unconscious men into custody. That left the sheriff herself and her one deputy to step into the kitchen.

"Hello, Sheriff," Hunter called out as she entered. "Welcome to the party."

The sheriff's mouth quirked into a smile. "I see I'm a little late for all the festivities," she retorted, glancing at the two men bound on the floor. "But better late than never." She nodded at each of the assemblage in turn. "Miss Sage. Miss Forest. Mister Creed." She paused on Scarlett. "I don't believe we've met—I'm Sheriff Watkins."

"Scarlett Quinn. I'm an old friend of Cookie's, just popped in for a visit," Scarlett replied, stepping forward and offering her hand. Cookie was pleased that she'd even remembered to call her "Cookie" rather than her usual "CJ." Not that the initials didn't still match, but it was easier to keep things simple.

Watkins smiled again. "Welcome to Hancock, Miss Quinn," she said as they shook. "I'd say you've chosen an interesting time to visit, but then with Ms. James it seems like that's always the case." The way she said it was half admiring and half amused. Cookie was glad that she didn't hear a trace of suspicion in the older woman's voice. She liked Sheriff Watkins, and didn't want the sheriff thinking that she was deliberately causing trouble.

It was just that trouble seemed to follow her.

That thought made her glance over at Dylan, who caught her eye, and she thought she saw a hint of amusement in his expression before his face returned to his previous blank slate. So he'd remembered their conversation as well, but things with him were still not right. She hoped she could fix that. And soon.

"We'll get this refuse out of your hair," Watkins said, waving a hand at the two captives. She frowned at Hunter and Cookie. "If you want to take the lead on interrogating them, be my guest."

Cookie only had to share a single quick look with Hunter before they both nodded. "Oh, absolutely," she replied. "We'll be right behind you."

"Actually, why don't I help you get them there now," Hunter offered, stooping to grab Mr. Smuggler off the floor. He hoisted the unconscious criminal onto his shoulder like a sack of flour and stood with a slight grunt, then turned and headed for the back door. Dylan beat him there, and held it open for him.

Watkins glanced at her phone. "Looks like the crime scene investigator is on his way," she said. "Ms. Sage, can you make sure he has unrestricted access to your property for the next hour or so?"

Winter visibly swallowed, but nodded as she eyed one of her more suspicious looking jars.

"Thank you." Watkins and her deputy wrestled the

other man up, and between them they hauled him out as well, leaving just Cookie, Winter, Rain, Scarlett, and Dylan.

"Well, I'm glad to see them gone," Winter said, grabbing the herb jar. After shoving it into a cabinet, she locked it, and then stole a quick, worried glance at Cookie. "Those crooks, I mean. I'm going to have scrub the entire place and use a smudge stick to erase any lingering traces of their negative energy. She shuddered a little at the thought, and Cookie felt a wave of sympathy for her. It wasn't Winter's fault the smugglers had chosen to invade her shop and make it their temporary meeting place.

Rain frowned. "I can't believe Anthony did this to me!" she burst out suddenly. "I don't know what's wrong with that man." She absentmindedly adjusted the towel tucked around her.

Cookie raised an eyebrow, her attention focused on her mother's unclothed state. "What did happen, exactly?" she asked Rain. "We found your clothes all over the lawn. At first I thought you were just… indisposed."

Scarlett smothered a laugh, but Rain only scowled more fiercely. "That's what I thought, too!" she snapped. "Or at least where I thought we were headed. Anthony showed up shortly after Scarlett and Dylan left. I thought he was there for some afternoon delight"—her lips twitched in a smile for a second before morphing into something between a scowl and a pout—"but when I started stripping he didn't follow suit. Instead he grabbed me, but not in the fun way, and then this car pulled up and the next thing I knew, Anthony and some thug were hustling me into it." She looked away, blinking rapidly.

Cookie's heart lurched as she imagined her mother's terror, but forced herself to pretend not to notice that she was near tears. If Rain started crying, she'd never get the full story out.

"Anthony had grabbed a towel off the line, I guess," she continued, "and he wrapped it around me before we got in the car. But that was the only nice thing he did for me. Can you imagine?" She waved a hand at her own barely concealed body. "To pass up all this?" She shook her head in disbelief. "The boy must need Viagra or something."

Cookie couldn't help but smile. She could see that her mother was upset, and hurt, and probably still feeling the aftereffects of the scare she'd had. But if Rain was already making cracks like that, Cookie suspected she'd be fine.

And one thing that would help would be knowing those men were behind bars for good. With that in mind, Cookie took a step back toward the door. "I'd better head to the station and help Hunter question them," she said as she went. "Are you guys okay here?"

"We're fine," Scarlett assured her, reaching out and hugging Rain and Winter to her. "We'll stay and help Winter clean up after the crime scene investigator is done, then Dylan will bring me and Rain back to the inn. Right?"

The others all nodded, and it was clear that Winter and Rain were relieved to let Scarlett take charge. Cookie again felt a burst of gratitude that her best friend had chosen now to stop by. She smiled, and Scarlett smiled back, the two of them on the same wavelength as always. Then Cookie glanced at Dylan, who stepped over to get the door for her.

"I'll make sure they get home safe," he assured her as she stepped through.

"I know you will," she told him. "Thanks."

He nodded, but as he shut the door behind her, Cookie couldn't help feeling a pang like she'd lost something. Dylan was looking out for her mom and Scarlett and Winter. Of course he was, because he was a good guy. But he hadn't added anything personal for her, and he still hadn't smiled at her. Not since he'd seen her in Hunter's arms.

Squaring her shoulders, Cookie marched toward the sheriff's office. Compared to dealing with her complicated love life, grilling a bunch of hardened drug smugglers would be a walk in the park.

24.

"**I** 'M BEAT," COOKIE murmured.

"Can't imagine why," Hunter teased. He yelped slightly when she poked him in the side, but was still chuckling as she rested her head against his arm again.

It was evening, the end of what had certainly been a very long day. They'd only gotten back from the station an hour ago, and they'd eaten a very nice pasta primavera Rain had prepared, complete with side salad and fresh-baked bread.

"For my saviors," she'd said, beaming when she'd served them. Apparently fearing for her life made Rain want to feed people. Not that Cookie was complaining. After that she'd sat and chatted with Scarlett a little bit, unwinding, catching up, and enjoying the fact that her best friend was there, even if it was in the midst of insanity. But now Scarlett was in her room on a conference call and Rain was cleaning up, or possibly in her hippie hideout, smoking up. Cookie could hardly blame her mother, given what she'd been through. There were far worse ways to cope with being kidnapped than getting high.

That meant Cookie and Hunter were left to their own devices. So now they were curled up together on the back porch swing, relaxing and digesting both their meal and the day's events.

Things at the station had gone well, better than Cookie had expected. They hadn't gotten much out of the drug runners, of course. Those who were conscious had refused to talk or even give their names, and Cookie and Hunter fully expected they'd be lawyered-up by morning. Their boss, Mr. Smuggler, wasn't talking either, but for a different reason.

"Broken nose, broken orbital ridge, cracked skull, heavy concussion," had been the doctor's report. "What hit him?"

"I did," Cookie had replied, daring the man to say anything else. He hadn't. Instead, he gulped and raised the clipboard in his hands as if he was half afraid she'd start in on him next. Hunter had stepped in, explaining that the man had been threatening innocent lives and that Cookie had beaned him with a heavy glass jar in self-defense.

"Well, he's not going to be talking any time soon," the doctor had concluded, shaking his head. Cookie didn't feel the least bit guilty about what she'd done. The guy had deserved it. Besides, he was still alive. If she'd had her gun handy, she would've shot him.

They'd hit the jackpot with Anthony, however. As Cookie had guessed, the lobsterman hadn't been a true member of the drug smugglers' crew. He'd been hired, like Jimmy Calder, to let them use his traps for their smuggling runs. With Jimmy dead and the smugglers arrested, Anthony had been only too happy to turn state's evidence against the crooks, and to spill his guts about everything he knew. Which, it turned out, included what exactly had happened to Jimmy.

"Everything was going fine," Anthony had told them miserably, huddled in his chair in the interrogation room. "We were pulling in good money, and we weren't really doing anything different than we normally did, 'cept we were hauling in drugs 'stead of lobsters." He shrugged. "I figured if I didn't, somebody else would, so why not make some cash off it, right?"

Neither Cookie nor Hunter replied to that as they glared at him across the table.

He dropped his gaze to his feet, but continued after a minute. "Jimmy thought the same. He wasn't too thrilled about the drugs, mind you, but he was happy for the money." He squirmed in his seat. "He kinda needed a lot of it, and fast."

That time Cookie nodded. "For his medical bills," she filled in. "And the trip he and his wife were going to take."

Anthony looked like he was on the verge of tears, and despite herself, Cookie felt a little sorry for him. The guy had definitely gotten in over his head. "Yeah, he was so excited about that. It was all he could talk about. And he was almost there, too. He almost made it."

"So what went wrong?" Hunter asked. Cookie was glad someone was able to keep them on track, because she'd been about ready to bawl herself, thinking about Jimmy and the fact that Leslie and Jimmy's dog was still waiting for him.

Anthony scowled. "The Coast Guard," he replied. "Jimmy and I were both out after dusk collecting the latest shipments, you know? And I saw the Coast Guard pass me by. I'd already hauled up one of my traps, though, and I had my running lights off and my engine down while I stowed it, so they didn't see me. Zipped right on by." He sighed. "Jimmy wasn't so lucky."

"The Coast Guard saw him?" Cookie asked.

"Yeah, saw him and told him to stop whatever he was doing since you're not supposed to be hauling traps after dark," Anthony replied. "I heard it all clear as day. Jimmy panicked, pitched his trap overboard, drugs and all. The Coast Guard boarded him, but they must've not found anything, 'cause after a quick search they let him go. But they warned him not to be out so late without lights or they'd ticket him, maybe impound his boat."

That had made sense to Cookie. At night, on the open water, the chances of someone running into you were pretty slim. But here by the islands most boats stuck to the established channels, and if you were near those and running dark there was a much bigger risk of collision. And two boats slamming into each other, either or both going full speed, was a sure-fire recipe for disaster.

She could guess the rest of the story. "He told the smugglers what happened, and instead of being pleased he hadn't gotten caught and put the whole operation at risk, they killed him for losing that one trap's worth of drugs," she said. "I'm right, aren't I?"

Anthony nodded. "He told them to take the cost out of his share," he said, near tears again thinking about his friend, "but they just said 'we do not tolerate failure.' Then they killed him." His resolve broke and the large man was unable to hold back his grief.

Cookie and Hunter gave him a minute before Hunter asked the six-million-dollar question. "Do you know what they did with Jimmy's body?"

As it turned out, Anthony did know. That old naval battery hadn't been a random choice. It was their favorite meeting spot. It was where he and Jimmy had always gone to hand off the drugs, and so it was where they'd shot Jimmy. And then they'd tied a rope around his body and dumped him down the hole at the center of the old gun placement in case they needed him again.

"Like if they wanted to send his hand along as a warning," Cookie had said. Still, even thinking about that grisly package, she'd had to fight hard not to grin, and Hunter had been much the same. Because if Jimmy's body was still there, they had the smugglers red-handed, not just for drugs, kidnapping, and assault with a deadly weapon, but for first-degree murder, too.

As a result, she'd been feeling pretty good when they left and headed back toward the inn. And she still was now, filled with the satisfaction of knowing this case was nearly at an end. Sheriff Hawkins and her team were handling Jimmy's remains and talking to his wife. Cookie knew the smugglers would get what was coming to them, that Jimmy would at least get some justice, and his wife would get some closure. But her satisfaction was now mingled with fatigue from everything she'd been through and the after-effects of the adrenaline rush from the confrontation at Winter's shop. So Cookie was content to just sit there, leaning against Hunter and rocking gently in the evening breeze as she gazed at the churning sea.

She yawned, and punched Hunter again when he laughed at her.

"Hey, stop beating on your partner," he said softly, capturing her fist in his hand. She struggled to pull free for a second, then gave up and rested her hand against his chest instead.

"Former partner," she reminded him sleepily, and he harrumphed in reply.

"Didn't feel like it today," he said after a second. "Felt like old times, actually."

"Yeah?" Cookie had let her eyes drift shut, but now she blinked one open to peer blearily up at him. "When did we ever pull a drug sting that involved confronting the dealers alone and unarmed?"

"You know what I mean," he chided her, but gently.

"We were a team today. Like we used to be."

Cookie couldn't argue that. "I'm glad you were here," she said instead.

"So am I." He tightened his grip on her, but not uncomfortably so. In fact, the pressure was nice. Comforting. Protective. "You scared me today, you know." His voice was soft and deep, a rumble she felt against her cheek and ear.

"I was scared too," she admitted. "Especially when he pulled that gun."

"Yeah." Hunter's heart was racing under her cheek as he gasped for breath. "I thought for a second I'd lost you."

"Nope, just a jar of Winter's best jam," she answered, but the joke fell flat. "Trust me," she added, "I was as relieved he missed as you were."

Hunter pulled back slightly, and reached down with one hand to take her chin and tilt her head so he could look at her. "I don't know what I'd do if anything happened to you," he told her, all the emotion he usually kept locked away pouring out in his rough voice and tender gaze.

"Well, I'll do my best to keep you from having to find out," she managed to reply, going for a lighter tone, but her words came out hoarse instead as tears burned her eyes. She tried to blink them away, hoping he hadn't noticed.

The smile Hunter gave her said he had, but that he didn't mind. "I'd appreciate it," was all he said.

Then he leaned forward and planted a soft kiss on her forehead, just the barest brush of his lips against her skin. But Cookie felt it like a bolt of lightning, the electricity shooting right through her all the way to her toes. And later, when they both finally succumbed to their weariness and crawled back inside and upstairs to their respective bedrooms, the memory of it burned in her still.

25.

"**H**EY."

Cookie glanced up, surprised. She and Hunter were sitting at the dining room table, but instead of food it was covered with papers. Specifically, new details on the case. Like Anthony's plea bargain and confession, the discovery of Jimmy Calder's body and the mug shots on the drug smugglers. All of them had been found in the system, mostly for smaller drug charges and things like assault and assault with a deadly weapon. Friendly bunch.

Cookie had been so focused on everything in front of her that she hadn't heard the front door open, or any footsteps. So she was shocked to find Dylan standing in the doorway, a wide, flat square box balanced on one hand. "Hey!" she replied, leaning back and smiling at him. He was definitely a sight for sore eyes, or any eyes for that matter, in his worn-soft gray T-shirt and equally worn blue jeans, his dark hair just a little mussed by the evening breeze. "What's going on? Sorry I haven't called, it's just been—" she gestured at the chaos on the table. "A little crazy."

"Yeah, I figured." They hadn't spoken at all since the events at the tea shop, and Cookie felt bad about that, even though it had only been yesterday. She should have made more of an effort. Although, she'd barely even seen Scarlett today, between her following up on the case and Scarlett keeping abreast of her law firm's activities. Scarlett was definitely one of those people who was never fully off the job even when she was on vacation.

The clattering of dishes drew her attention toward the kitchen where Scarlett was currently helping Rain clean up from dinner. But in the next moment, the door swung open and the two of them wandered back in.

"Howdy, stranger," Scarlett said, striding over to Dylan and tossing an arm over his shoulder like they'd been friends forever. "Whatcha got there?" She reached for the box.

"Pie," he answered, shifting and stretching to keep it out of her reach. "I was hoping Cookie might have a few minutes to step out with me, watch the sunset, and enjoy some dessert."

"How about she gets the sunset and I get the pie?" Scarlett countered, using his neck as a pivot to swing around and grab for the box again. "What kind is it?"

"Blueberry," Dylan answered, laughing and performing what looked almost like a dance move to keep the box away from her. "I'll save you a piece."

Watching the two of them was like watching a cross

between performance art, dance, and a comedy routine, and Cookie couldn't help but chuckle.

"Oh, fine." Scarlett stopped lunging and pouted instead, making herself instantly adorable. Cookie had witnessed her use those moves on many a man in her personal life, always to devastating effect. The fact that Dylan only laughed again and tousled her hair in a big-brother sort of way both amazed Cookie and impressed her. And judging by the knowing look Scarlett shot her over Dylan's broad shoulders, her best friend felt the same way.

"Go," Hunter grumbled, apparently throwing Dylan a bone. "It's not like the paperwork won't still be here when you get back."

"Are you sure?" Cookie asked, already sliding from her chair. "Because if it were to magically disappear or be completed before I returned, that'd be like Christmas come early."

"Bah, humbug," her ex-partner grumbled back. His eyes were slits as he said it, but Cookie ignored his jealousy and turned away before he could change his mind.

"Right, let's get out of here quick, before Scarlett makes another try for the pie," she suggested, linking her arm with Dylan's and leading him toward the kitchen. "How about out back?"

"Sounds good," he agreed, letting her guide him. Together they traipsed through the kitchen, pausing just long enough to snag a pair of plates and utensils before heading out the back door into the yard.

The sun was indeed just starting to set, casting alternating fingers of shadow and streamers of light everywhere. The yard had been transformed into a beautiful, almost haunting setting, with the inn as the backdrop and the water stretching away as the main view. Looking out over the ocean as it glowed and shimmered was breathtaking, and Cookie froze, drinking it all in for a second. Then, beaming herself, she led Dylan over to the lawn chairs and the little table between them. The same one they'd used for their make-up picnic dinner that felt like ages ago.

"Look familiar?" she asked as she set down the plates and eased onto one of the chairs. "I think maybe we've been here before." She grinned. "Only this time you brought the food."

"I figured it was my turn," he answered, taking the other seat. He carefully opened the pie box, and a deliciously sweet berry aroma wafted out.

"Wow, where did you get that?" Cookie asked. There was a bakery in town, but while their cookies were decent, and their breads were good, she'd never seen anything there that looked or smelled like this.

Now it was Dylan's turn to grin. "So you remember Mrs. Ledger?" he asked, his attention on carving two large slices and setting them on the plates.

It took Cookie a second, then it came to her. "The one with the flooded basement?"

"One and the same." Finishing his task, he closed the

box again, set the cake-server atop it, and lifted his plate, fork already in hand. "Turns out she is a pie-maker extraordinaire. I was over there today to make sure everything had dried out okay, and she presented me with two fresh-baked pies. This one and an apple. I kept the apple."

"Hmm, so I only rate blueberry?" Cookie frowned, or tried to. "Guess I've got something to work up to, then." But when she took a bite of her pie, the tart blueberries mixing perfectly with the sugar of the filling and the flaky, buttery texture of the crust, she felt like she'd already hit the jackpot.

They ate in silence for a few minutes, just enjoying the amazing dessert, the incredible scenery, and each other's company. "This is really, really nice," Cookie said finally, after she'd polished off her piece and set the plate back down. "Thank you."

"You're welcome," he said, meeting her gaze. There was a comfortable silence as they watched each other. Then his attention shifted to her mouth, and she leaned in toward him, lips parting slightly.

But he pulled away.

For half a second, she thought he'd missed her intent, or that she was misinterpreting his reaction. But he was staring at his empty plate, heavily invested in using his fork to scrape up practically nonexistent scraps of pie, and most definitely avoiding meeting her eyes.

"Um, okay." Cookie righted herself. "Is something wrong? Do I have blueberry between my teeth? Is Rain staring at us through the kitchen window? What's going on?"

Dylan sighed and lowered his plate. "I'm sorry," he said after a second, finally glancing up at her again. In the deepening twilight, his eyes were almost completely gray, but a lighter shade than she'd seen when he was angry. "But I don't think this is going to work."

"Wait, what?" She was staring, she knew, but she couldn't help it. Her stomach had just lurched and now it was knotting up. "You don't think this is going to work? You mean us? Why not? I thought...I mean, sure, we've hit a few bumps in the road—"

"Each of those bumps being a dead body," he pointed out.

She waved that off. "What about dinner the other night? That was nice—up until we got interrupted. And being on your boat, that was nice too—until Dickie happened. And on the island, that was great—until we found the drugs. And—"

"That's kind of my point," Dylan interrupted. He reached out and caught her hands in his, his fingers rough but warm. Reassuring. "I really like you, Cookie," he said, and he definitely wasn't looking away now.

"Yeah? Well, I really like you too, Dylan," she replied, matching his gaze. "So what's the problem?"

"The problem is that I'm not the only one you like," he answered bluntly, and now it was her turn to look away. "Or the only thing." He waited until she felt compelled to meet his gaze again before he continued. "I saw what happened between you and Hunter at the tea shop."

"Oh." Suddenly she felt small and stupid and horrible. And that pie that had been so delicious was now a lump in the pit of her stomach. "That."

"That." He shook his head. "Look, it was a scary situation, emotions were running high, you were almost killed. I get it. But you can't tell me you don't genuinely feel something for him."

A part of her, the part that wanted Dylan to stay, really wanted to tell him just that. But Cookie couldn't. Both because she didn't want to lie to him and because she couldn't lie to herself.

He just nodded. He didn't look angry, either. More resigned. "It's more than that, though," he continued slowly. "It's the job. I asked you before if you missed being an FBI agent. If you could really be happy here, with the inn, with me. And you said you yes."

"And I meant it," she insisted. But he was already shaking his head again.

"Maybe you wanted to mean it," he corrected gently. "Or maybe you even did mean it at the time. But I've seen you in action, remember? You love it."

Again, she couldn't deny that. Because she did love it. She loved the thrill, the danger, the power. It was when she felt most alive.

"I told you once that I wasn't the kind of guy who'd cut into an existing relationship," Dylan reminded her. "Even when it was just something that was starting out. I meant that. You told me then that you didn't have feelings for Hunter, but either you weren't being honest, you didn't realize them, or that's changed. Whichever it was, I can't keep seeing you as long as there's a chance you're into him. And I can't see you if you're going to be busy wishing you were back in the FBI with him instead of here with me."

He stood up and, leaning over, brushed a kiss across her forehead. Ironically, it was in almost exactly the same spot Hunter had kissed her the night before. But whereas Hunter's kiss had electrified Cookie, Dylan's now felt like an icicle piercing right down into her heart, freezing her into a numb shock.

"I'll be around," he promised. "You know that if you need me, I'm here. Plus, I'm hoping we're still friends, no matter what. And if things change… well, we can talk about this again, maybe. But until then, this is the way it's gotta be. I'm sorry."

Then he turned and walked away.

Cookie shifted to watch him go, his footsteps nearly silent as he moved. She wanted to call him back, to say that she did care about him, that she did like it here, that she wanted things to work out between them. But she knew that wasn't being fair to him. Or to her. He'd made it clear where he stood, and she had to respect that, even if a part of her felt like curling up and crying her eyes out, or cursing and breaking everything in sight.

Because another part of her knew that by stepping back, he'd actually given her the space to decide for herself exactly what she wanted.

And whom.

26.

"**W**OW." SCARLETT WRAPPED her arms around Cookie and held her for a minute before pulling back slightly to study her face. "Good for him."

"What?" Cookie thwacked her best friend on the arm. "You're supposed to be on my side."

"CJ, I'm always on your side, you know that," her friend replied in a serious tone. "But there isn't a 'your side' or 'his side' here."

"He dumped me!" Cookie exclaimed. She grabbed the nearest pillow and shoved it against her face to muffle any other awkward announcements she decided to scream out at the top of her lungs with both her mother and Hunter nearby.

Scarlett wasn't having any of that, though, and wrestled the pillow away from her, tossing it back onto the bed behind them. "No, he didn't," she corrected firmly. "He told you he couldn't be with someone who wasn't sure what or who they wanted, and that he was giving you space until you figured that out. And I, for one, think that's a pretty gutsy thing to do." She smiled and patted Cookie on the back. "If he didn't have my seal of approval before, he sure as heck does now."

"Yeah, great, except now that you've cleared him to date me, he doesn't want to." Cookie held up her hands. "I know, I know, he does still want to. He's just not going to. Not until I've got my head on straight." She grumbled and pounded her fists on the bed. "Why is it the one time I'd rather have a needy, selfish guy, I get Mr. Noble?"

Her friend peered at her. "Are you honestly telling me you'd like him better if he didn't consider your feelings?"

"Well, maybe for a few minutes," Cookie mumbled, then sighed. "Fine. No, not really. Not the morning after, anyway." She caught her friend's grin. "Shut up." She smacked Scarlett again, but this time her bestie grabbed the discarded pillow and used it to fend off the blow. Of course then Cookie had to snatch up another pillow and in seconds they were having a good old-fashioned pillow fight, just like they used to back when they'd roomed together.

Ten minutes and a bunch of good thwacks later, they both collapsed onto the bed, staring up at the ceiling, their heads touching. "Feel better?" Scarlett asked.

"Some," Cookie admitted. "Thanks, Scar."

"Always." Her friend lifted up to smile down at her. And then bopped her full in the face with the pillow.

"What? Why, you—oh, it's on!" And they went at it

again.

Which, right now, was exactly what Cookie needed.

A little while later, after they'd both caught their breath, she and Scarlett headed back downstairs. Rain must have heard them coming, because she was standing in the hallway waiting for them. And she wasn't alone.

"Sweetie, you remember Hale, don't you?" Rain declared as they approached. She was grinning like she'd won the lottery, and the way she had her arm wrapped protectively around the courier's waist, she clearly felt she had. For his part, Hale looked a lot more cognizant than the last time they'd met, and just as happy to be cuddled up against Rain as she was with him.

"Sure, hi," Cookie said, waving as she reached the ground floor. "Oh, and this is my friend Scarlett. Scarlett, this is Hale."

"Hey, nice to meet you," Hale said, smiling at them both. "Wow, I've gotta stop by this place more often," he joked, which made Rain frown for half a second. But then he gave her an affectionate squeeze and she visibly relaxed again.

"What, is it a party?" Hunter's voice called out as he strolled in from the living room. Cookie noticed that he was wearing his "boating" outfit again, board shorts and tank top. Had he been wearing that earlier? She was pretty sure he hadn't.

"Hunter, you remember Hale," Rain told him, looking delighted as the two men shook hands. "Hale, this is Hunter. You met him the last time you were here.

The FBI agent?"

"I did?" Hale looked a little puzzled, but then he shrugged good-naturedly. "Hey, sorry, dude. I'm a little fuzzy about that visit. You know how it goes."

Hunter didn't, really, but he nodded anyway. "Sure, sure. So what're you kids up to tonight?"

"We're going skinny-dipping down at this cove Hale knows," Rain said, giggling like a schoolgirl. Then she eyed Hunter up and down and her grin turned predatory. "Want to join us?"

"Hey, sure, y'all are all welcome," Hale agreed, and Cookie gave him credit for only letting his eyes roam over her and Scarlett for half a second. "The more the merrier."

"Oh, I'd love to," Scarlett said with impressive sincerity, "but I've got this call I've got to take." Sure enough her phone was ringing, and she waved goodbye as she turned and slid past them into the living room, already raising the phone to her ear.

"What about the two of you?" Rain asked Cookie and Hunter. "Nothing like a little naked night-swimming to clear your head."

Cookie glanced at Hunter, trying not to plead with her eyes. Fortunately, those years of partnering together had taught him how to interpret her looks at least half the time, and he shook his head.

"Thanks for the offer," he answered, "but I was actually thinking of taking Cookie out on the boat to look at the stars. Seems like a nice night for it."

"Oh?" If there was one thing about Rain, it was that she wasn't selfish. She was thrilled to know that someone she cared about might be getting lucky too. And that most definitely included Cookie. Which was why her grin got even wider now, and she practically dragged Hale toward the front door. "That sounds lovely. You two have a great time," she called over her shoulder, winking broadly at Cookie as she left. "I'll want to hear *all* about it in the morning." Then she and Hale exited, though not before Cookie got to see her mom grabbing her new beau's butt in an iron grip.

"I'm going to be in therapy until I'm ninety if she keeps this up," Cookie stated, shaking her head as if that could clear away the image. Then she glanced up at Hunter. "Good save, though. Thanks."

"Ah, actually, I was serious," he said. "What do you say? Nice night, clear sky, stars, boat, water?" He held out his arm to her like an old-fashioned gentleman.

For a second, Cookie just stared at him. Was this really Hunter? Her Hunter, who was always so sleek and fashionable looking, whether suited-up for work or wearing something club-worthy on his downtime? And now here he was looking like a surfer dude and asking her to go stargazing with him? He still had his arm up, and he looked serious, so finally she laughed and linked her arm through his.

"Yeah, sure, why not?" she said. "I mean, I would be delighted, kind sir." She glanced down at what she was wearing and realized that the bikini, shorts, and halter-tied overshirt were probably perfect for this. Besides, it was just Hunter.

Which didn't explain the butterflies flitting about in her stomach as she let him lead her out.

"Okay, so this is nice," she admitted an hour later. They'd walked down to the dock and then taken the cigarette boat, which she was steadfastly refusing to ask Hunter about, out onto the open water, being careful to avoid active shipping lanes. Then they'd turned off the engine and just let the boat drift a little with the mild current as they lay on their backs on the forward couches that Hunter had extended, making them completely flat, like a king-size bed right there on the deck.

It was perfectly clear tonight, and they were far enough away from both the island and shore that no lights interfered. The position gave them an amazing view of the velvety sky and its panorama of twinkling, glittering little lights.

"More than nice," he said. They were lying side by side, their hands linked together, their shoulders just brushing up against each other. For Cookie that meant Hunter was a solid, reassuring shape in her peripheral vision, calm and steady. Just like always. "I thought you could use a little escape."

"Yeah." She sighed. "I guess you heard about what happened with Dylan?" She wasn't entirely sure how much any of the others had overheard from inside the house.

"Not anything specific," he answered. "But I

couldn't help but notice that when you came back in alone, you looked like someone'd just shot your dog." He shrugged, which sent a minor ripple through the couches. "I'm guessing it didn't go well."

A sharp laugh tore out of her. "You could say that. He thinks I miss the FBI too much to be happy here."

"Is he right?" Hunter squeezed her fingers, and she tilted her head so that she and Hunter were eye to eye, only inches apart. "I'm serious, Charlie," he said, reverting to the nickname he knew her by. "You loved being an agent. Are you really ready to give that up for good?"

Since he was being serious about the question, she gave the answer real, proper consideration. "I don't know," she admitted after a minute. "I thought I was, for a bit. But I have to admit I did get kind of stir crazy. Then all sorts of weird crimes started going on here, and I was fine again." She let herself smile a little. "I guess that's not exactly normal, right? That I'm only happy when I'm dealing with dead people?"

His fingers tightened on hers once again, and she noticed it was warm and comforting. "No," he told her. "It's not about dead people and you know it. You're happiest when you're trying to set things right." For a second he was quiet, gently stroking the back of her hand with his thumb. Then he spoke again, and his voice was deep, and low, and filled with old pain. "Did I ever tell you why I joined the Bureau?"

She could only shake her head. Something about his

voice, his mood, his touch had her completely entranced.

"When I was a kid," Hunter went on, "I had this friend, Wally. Wally Brett. We were like brothers, we were so close. We did everything together. And his dad, Mr. Brett, he was like the best guy ever. My own dad, he...wasn't always there for me. But Mr. Brett sure was. I always knew any time I was hurting, or confused, or scared, I could go over there, and he'd welcome me, talk to me, or give me whatever space I needed. But he was always ready to help."

He paused for a second, and now his voice was even more gravelly than before. "When we were twelve, I was over at Wally's one night. His dad asked us if we'd eaten all the ice cream. He pretended to be mad about it but we knew he wasn't really, and then he said he was going to go out and get some more." There was a definite hitch to Hunter's voice, and he was carefully not looking at Cookie now. "He got mugged on the way home. They took his wallet, his watch, his wedding ring. Then they shot him in the head. For no reason. He'd never hurt anybody, didn't have it in him. I can't imagine he put up a fight or even talked back, but they shot him anyway."

His grip started to hurt her fingers, but Cookie didn't try to pull away. Instead she squeezed back, letting him know she was there for him.

"They never found who did it," Hunter continued after a minute, his voice ragged and his breathing harsh and heavy. "No clue. And I just... I couldn't believe that this good man, this *really* good man, could get killed and whoever did it would just get away with it. I decided right then I was going to be a cop so I could catch bad guys like that." He sighed. "But when I got to the police academy, I found out that while there're some really good cops, there're some really bad ones too. And there's a lot of politics, red tape and a lot of noise complaints and parking violations and all that crap. I wanted to go after the real bad guys, not jaywalkers or ravers. That's when I applied to the Bureau instead. So I could make a difference."

"I—I had no idea," Cookie managed after he'd fallen silent. "Hunter, I'm so sorry."

He glanced over at her, and even in the dim starlight she could see his eyes were glassy with tears. "I didn't tell you that to make you feel sorry for me," he explained. "I told you so you'd know why I do what I do. What *we* do. Because I can't stand to see bad people get away with hurting good ones. And I don't think you can, either." He reached out with his free hand and stroked her cheek. A delightful tingle of electricity raced through Cookie as he said, "The question is can you really sit back and let other people go after those bad people instead of doing it yourself?"

Cookie froze, staring into his warm brown gaze. She already knew the answer to that, and so did he. She'd never been any good at sitting back and letting other people take control. But that didn't mean she could only be happy in the FBI. In some ways, her time on the island had been even better than her tenure with the

Bureau, because she'd still been helping people and catching crooks, but she'd been doing it with a lot more freedom and a lot less bureaucracy. It just meant she still needed to be able to help people and stand up for the law, no matter her official title.

And right now, the person who needed her help the most was her partner and friend. Because he'd dredged up one of his most painful memories—for her. Propping herself up on one arm, she leaned over and draped herself across Hunter's chest, hugging him tight. His arm went around her and he hugged her back, the pair of them lying there for a moment, neither of them saying anything.

Then she pulled back and lifted herself up so she could see him. They were inches apart again, but no longer side by side. Now they were facing each other. And their lips were so close his breath was warm upon her cheek. He leaned forward that last little bit, and his lips brushed against hers.

And even as she felt herself respond, pushing back to increase the contact, feeling that electricity spark through her again, Cookie couldn't help but wonder, *what do we do now?*

THE END

Find out more about Lucy Quinn's latest release at
www.lucyquinnauthor.com

Secret Seal Isle Mysteries
A New Corpse in Town
Life in the Dead Lane
A Walk on the Dead Side
Any Way You Bury It
Death is in the Air
Signed, Sealed, Fatal, I'm Yours

Lucy Quinn is the brainchild of New York Times bestselling author Deanna Chase and USA Today bestselling author Violet Vaughn. Having met over a decade ago in a lampwork bead forum, the pair were first what they like to call "show wives" as they traveled the country together, selling their handmade glass beads. So when they both started writing fiction, it seemed only natural for the two friends to pair up with their hilarious laugh-out-loud cozy mysteries. At least they think so. Now they travel the country, meeting up in various cities to plan each new Lucy Quinn book while giggling madly at themselves and the ridiculous situations they force on their characters. They very much hope you enjoy them as much as they do.

Deanna Chase, is a native Californian, transplanted to the slower paced lifestyle of southeastern Louisiana. When she isn't writing, she is often goofing off with her husband in New Orleans, playing with her two shih tzu dogs, or making glass beads.

Violet Vaughn lives in coastal New Hampshire where she spends most mornings in the woods with her dogs, summer at the ocean, and winters skiing in the mountains of Maine.

Made in the USA
Middletown, DE
12 July 2021